THE
SHATTERED
FABERGE
EGG

SPECIAL EDITION

TONYA MCBEAN

Inks and Bindings
888-290-5218
www.inksandbindings.com
orders@inksandbindings.com

Contents

CHAPTER 1

There are parts of Mammoth Cave that are shrouded in pitch black. Even with flashlights, one can feel the oppressive weight of the blackness all around. We were encompassed by it, and to truly take in the experience, our tour guide asked us to turn off our flashlights. Utter darkness surrounded me, and for a moment, I was reminded of my life in the past. It felt just like this; squeezed into a tight spot and blinded by darkness.

At that moment, in the depths of my consciousness, my mind drifted to the feeling of being punched awake at three in the night. He was agitated, and his blows woke me from my sleep. I felt another blow land on my ear and pain seared through my head in a state of disorientation. I tried to roll out of the way, but he was faster. Another blow landed on my nose, and blood began running down my cheek. Tears streamed down my face from the abuse.

I covered my face with my hands and scrambled out of bed. It was dark and I felt tiny droplets of blood falling from my nose. Bracing myself for the next punch, I turned, but I felt his hand slap me instead. Fear gripped me. Attacking in my sleep was vicious, even for him.

"STOP. STOP IT," I screamed.

I had to get out of here. He might try to kill me one day. Why hadn't someone warned me about what I was getting into?

My emotions were all over the place, and I was exhausted from walking on eggshells, trying so hard to step without cracking them. Never knowing what would set him off, I could never sleep peacefully.

I despise myself for closing my eyes, for allowing it to happen again. I had refused to fight back, but how could I? How could I hit him? I began to convince myself that it wasn't as bad as it seemed. I would whisper to myself, "This one was not that bad." It would prepare me for what the day would bring.

The pain was difficult to bear, but the thought of what he was doing to me felt worse than the actual blows upon my skin. No amount of physical violence could equal the mental pain I was feeling.

The damage to my personal belongings: clothing, furniture, and pictures seemed like a cruel punishment, and caused further agony to my aching soul. I wondered what wrong I had done to cause someone to lash out at me so brutally. I wanted it to stop. But I could not fight back. I didn't know what to do or who to reach out to. If I did say something, the consequences would be too devastating. In a way, I was punishing myself for something that wasn't my fault.

Who would ever believe this was happening to me? Who would hear my pleas? I wanted even now to protect him, but he was hurting me, over and over. This assault lasted longer than the last, and I was struggling to bottle my anger and pain. Experiencing infuriation at him for so long that my anger imploded upon me, almost to the point of depression. Uncontrollably, I could not escape the grips of self-doubt.

Why me?

Would ever life a normal life again?

Did I do something to deserve this?

Was this my fault?

For me, spring was the most beautiful time of the year: an expression of how life can begin again after a long, dark season of bitter cold. Watching winter turn into spring–azaleas blooming in lush meadows–like life bursting forth all around.

Tonya McBean

I am a North Carolina girl, born to a Southern family in Asheville, and was brought up in a country club. My dad, Charles Stenson, worked hard as an attorney to provide a life of comfort for me and my older sister, Jill. Remembering how he would come home after a long day, give me a hug, and take me out to the fields to show me the beauty. His words would always be the same, "This is yours to enjoy, Kate. Always remember where you came from."

At the time, I never truly understood what he meant. It wasn't until many years later that I would uncover the meaning behind his words.

Dad's worth ethic was 'finish what you have to do, and do a better job than you're expected to do.' He believed that it was vital for him to put in his best and go above expectations. One of his defining characteristics was that he left things better than he found them.

Jill and I began working at the law office during the summers. None of our friends were working, but Dad thought it was important to pass on his work ethic to us at an early age. The pay was per hour, and we received payroll checks that we would have to cash out. This helped us learn the value of money at an early age.

One summer, Dad gave us a huge filing project to do. It was definitely a lot to manage, and he always tried to give us ways to prove ourselves. We had to manage the paperwork for almost a hundred clients and put it into their files in the firm's gigantic file room. We worked in the conference room, where all the paperwork was stacked. Jill and I were supposed to 'file the pile', one client at a time. "Pile of poo" was the name Jill gave it. We giggled and began.

The manila folders were large, and the huge paperclips made it hard to stack them. Jill and I decided to take all the paperclips off and then start the filing. We had barely made progress when the office manager walked in and nearly had a stroke after finding out what we had done. She was worried that we would spill soda on them. She literally ran to our dad and almost pulled off his suit coat as she dragged him down to the conference room to show him the mess we had made. In her mind, she was probably thinking, "You spoiled little brats! Look at what you've done!"

Dad never said a word to the office manager, but rather, spoke directly to us. "Fix this," he said in a serious tone. "Then finish what you started and do a good job," He added to emphasize his point. It took both of us several days to reorganize the files, but we got every paperclip back in place and placed each file where it belonged. Because of our mess that summer, we wound up working longer than dad had intended. The real satisfaction came when we finally finished the job, and went shopping with the money we had earned. I remember buying myself a popular brand purse.

Our upbringing really helped us develop integrity and a set of morally upright principles. I remember how the ticking clock was right outside the bookkeeper's office, and it made a loud punch when you pushed in your time card. Jill and I would often clock in or out for each other until Dad put a stop to it. He explained to us that nobody could punch your time card for you in real life.

Along with our time spent at work, we always spent time together as a family. Dad took us to lunch on the days we worked and always introduced us as his daughters, Jill and Kate. The way he took ownership of us as his offspring made us feel proud to have such a respectable person as our guardian and representative.

This pride meant that we respected our father deeply. When dad gave instructions, he only gave them once. We never questioned him or even considered going against what he had said. He never even yelled at us or raised his voice, because he knew that we didn't want to disappoint him and that was enough to keep us in line. On the rare occasions when I made him angry, he would say, "Kate, I love you, but I'm disappointed." It felt worse than any other form of disciplining.

Suddenly, the delicious smell of brewing coffee jolted me out of my daydream. The memories of time spent with my Dad were replaced by the usual sights and sounds of my morning routine.

It was quiet and peaceful today, and I could hear Jax in the kitchen making coffee. He liked his coffee stronger than I did, but he was stronger than I was so it made sense. I loved my husband, Jackson Lee Harper, and could not imagine life without him. He was self-confident, alert, and an accomplished news photographer with an award-winning career. Picture a confident man with a well-defined muscular physique. His dark hair added to his rugged charm with his piercing blue eyes that drew you in, reflecting both intensity and charm. He was a Texas boy, and he epitomizes the essence of a man's man. Everyday Jax made me fall in love with him all over again just by putting on jeans.

"Hey, Nugget, How about some coffee? I made it weak just like you like it. Jax said gleefully.

I rolled my eyes and laughed while he hugged me tightly and patted my behind, "I'm so glad you are my wife." Jax whispered in my ear.

No man had ever loved me as Jax did. When we hugged each other he wrapped me up in a bear hug and my face fit perfectly in the curve of his neck which smelled like sandalwood and soap. We lived in peace most of the time, unless one of us did something to irritate the other. In most cases, I would get flamed up, and thirty seconds later, we would be laughing as everything was forgotten. We had a very close relationship where I felt safe. There is nothing he would not do to protect me. It was comforting to have someone genuinely in love with me.

Relaxing on the chaise lounge and looking at the sunshine on a beautiful day, who would have thought that just a few years ago this kind of relaxation was impossible for me?

Back then, my life was filled with dread, fear, and loathing all at once. It was like a Faberge Egg, shining and beautiful on the outside. However, once you opened it, the insides were held together with duct tape, band-aids, and super glue. My life had been broken into pieces, but now, Jax was mending the hairline cracks, Emma and Jill were the duct tape keeping everything in place.

Suddenly, my cell phone rang. It was Jill. The relationship I had with my sister was much deeper than a typical sibling bond. Jill was a rock of stability, and she had always been there for me, no matter what. We were close friends and confidants, and I could tell her anything. During the darkest times of my past, I could always sense the glimmering light of my sister standing by me, wanting to do more to help, but respecting my boundaries. Where would I be without her?

"Hey there, Jill. What's up?" I asked.

"Travis and I are thinking about going to Keeneland in Lexington in April. Do you and Jax want to go?" she asked.

"Yes, of course, I want to go. I've never been to the horse races in Keeneland," I said.

"We have a plan to visit Sam and Shelby in the UK, then go to the races. Then we could go back to Mammoth Cave if you like," Jill said.

"That's not even funny. Let me call you back," I said.

Sam and Shelby (Travis and Jill's twins) had started attending the University of Kentucky, and we had visited them last year. As a family, we went to Mammoth Cave, which I was so excited to see. Having heard about the cool air inside the beautiful rock cave, I couldn't wait to peek inside. However, when we arrived, I realized that the tour was actually a hike inside the earth, 200 to 300 feet below the surface.

I expressed my apprehension to Jill, telling her that I had expected to walk in with my Starbucks and peek at the cave over a rail before leaving. However, Jill had already paid for the entire group to go on the tour. Jax, always prepared, pulled out an LED headlight headband from his backpack, as the warning sign said no backpacks, purses, or packages were allowed. He always lived by his motto of situational awareness.

Jill informed us that the tour would take two hours and warned us that we would have to squeeze into tight spaces within the cold, damp cave. I protested, saying, "I didn't even bring a coat because I didn't have one that matched this outfit."

We climbed down a long staircase, and I noticed the sparkle on the walls and floor, which I found fascinating. The tour guide explained that it was gypsum, which contains calcium sulfate.

Shelby said, "Only Aunt Kate would notice sparkles."

I asked Emma, Sam, and Shelby, "Which one of you thought it would be a good idea to take me caving?"

The guide led us past stalagmites and into the Rotunda Room, where he explained that Mammoth Cave was home to an endangered species of eyeless cave shrimp. I couldn't help but draw a parallel between myself and the cave shrimp, once blind to what was going on around me. I whispered to Jill that she was in danger of becoming endangered herself if she didn't get me out of there soon. The cave was a chilly 55 degrees and incredibly dark. I clung to Jax's belt loop, grateful for the light on his head. I'd follow him anywhere but this was a little much.

As we continued on the tour, the guide pointed out eroded sandstone in the Frozen Niagara Room, Cedar Sink, a massive sinkhole with a small river flowing into it, and Fat Man's Misery, a passageway that had been polished smooth by years of spelunking. Finally, we came to Bottomless Pit, which dropped 105 feet deep. I couldn't believe I had volunteered to go spelunking in this truly amazing and unique cave. The guide said that caves were nature's final frontier.

I quipped, "Hey, how much longer?" Jill nudged me, signaling me to be quiet.

Suddenly, my phone beeped with a notification from Emma's tweet: "Going to Keeneland horse races in April."

Jill comforted me, saying, "Don't worry, it'll get easier next year. You're a good mom."

Thinking back on my childhood, some of my fondest memories were when our mom, Suzanne, would pick Jill and me up from the country club in the late afternoon. Mom would always make sure to sneak the cook, Pearl, into the back seat of the Cadillac and drive her home. It was heartwarming to see how much Mom cared for Pearl, who had to walk a mile to the bus stop after a long day in the kitchen. Jill and I loved it because we knew Mom would always put something in the trunk for Pearl to give to her grandchildren. It was often items we no longer used, but it was very touching to see her give them to Pearl. It was a silent understanding borne from compassion. Mom would pop the trunk and Pearl would take the bag and not a word was said of the exchange.

Looking back at it now, we thank God for blessing us with a woman like our mother. Her steadying influence and godly guidance helped me to navigate the feelings of anguish and despair I never thought I would experience. She instilled within me the grace to maintain my composure in the most difficult of times, and visions of her elegance and demeanor would give me strength during my challenges, always reminding me of who I was and where I had come from. Her posture and dauntless gaze could bring peace and silence to a room full of conflict, a quality that I always aspired to achieve.

When our Father died, Mom had to handle all the funeral arrangements and tidy up the loose ends of his law practice. More than once, I saw her stand firm, eye-to-eye with powerful men who wanted something she was unwilling to give. I watched her negotiate with men who thought they were more proficient than her, and I saw them fall like flies in a trap as Mom outwitted them on every level.

Growing up, Mom had been brought up to believe that men made all of the decisions, but after being married to our father, she learned just how important is was to be involved in the decision- making process. This also ensured that both our parents accepted responsibility for their individual and collective decisions and could defend them if necessary.

Dad also invited Mom to accompany him to his office so she could learn about the business. She was a skillful organizer and helped him prepare his cases. This level of involvement gave her a thorough understanding of the firm and the actions she need to take after his death to ensure that everything continued to progress in a systematic manner.

Mom's strength and determination weren't just limited to the business world. She was a force to be reckoned with even at home. One, when I was four, Mom had been asking Dad to be home for dinner more often. She considered it important that he spent more time with the family each night instead of working. It was during this time that Dad ended up missing dinner with us for a week. When her patience finally ran out, Mom got Jill and me out of bed in our PJs, put us in the back of the Cadillac, and drove to Dad's office. He was still working, and to our surprise, she threw a brick right through the front window. Without another word, she drove us home and put us back to bed. The incident was never discussed again, but right after this, Dad began having dinner with us more often.

Mom was deeply in touch with her feminine side, and you could find her in heels with sweetness in her voice. Despite this, you could see the toughness in her personality. Her nails, hair, and make-up were always done in a Southern belle-meets-Junior League kind of way.

When Dad had his heart surgery, she remained by his side. She cared for him with tender and gentle love, even when he would lash out. They had been high school sweethearts and she loved him without question. I even remember her telling me that she knew he was the one she would marry at their very first meeting. I can always proudly claim that Dad's legacy was far more than a successful law practitioner with two daughters. His legacy was also his wife who treated him with respect and admiration, both at home and in public. Truly, their bond was one of special devotion and unparalleled love.

The bond I saw between Mom and Dad, I wanted in my own life. Their love and commitment, their companionship, their trust, and loyalty—it was special, rare, and truly desirable. I believed I could find love as they had, but little did I know that I would end up in a romance that was in stark contrast to my expectations. Where I expected love and compassion, I found darkness and despair that made me question my own sanity.

It was ironic, really. I had grown up in a home that practiced what it preached. My parents had taught me to tell the truth by being truthful themselves. They showed me how to respect other people by showing respect. They showered me with love, so I may be enabled to love others. I could understand genuine, heartfelt love, because I had experienced it. I had been loved.

So how could I become entangled in such a web of deceit, violence, rage, and dysfunction? How could I, a properly trained southern belle, become the object of scorn and ridicule by one of the wealthiest and most influential families in Asheville?

It may seem as though I am rambling now, always looping back to the same thoughts of my past, but it is difficult to rid yourself of something so sinister. Nothing is worse than being afraid and cloaked in fear. There were years when I couldn't relax, simply because I forgot how. My life had become unmanageable. Eventually, the darkness and fear became so omnipresent that I began to believe it would never lift.

I am so thankful for the way my life turned out despite the downward spiral. As far as my own judgment is concerned, it is clear to me now that I made the right decisions by changing everything in my life. I live in a different world now, where I feel safe–a place where I can relax and find peace.

Nevertheless, I sometimes dream about the past. The dreams are often vivid, where I am trapped once more, begging for him to stop hurting me. Begging him to stop even as he lets out his anger and rage upon my physical self. Other times, I dream that he is normal, and there was nothing wrong in the first place. After every dream, I wake up confused, even fearful sometimes, but there is always something I am relieved about.

It is not my present reality.

CHAPTER 2

Like most people, there are moments from my past that I can't remember or simply don't want to remember. But regardless of what has happened before, I am a firm believer that I am where I am meant to be. My past does not define me, nor does it determine my future.

During my previous marriage, I clung to the hope that things would eventually improve, even though the reality was far from it. Despite the chaos and dysfunction, there were certain events that strengthened my resolve to push through and come out the other side.

One day, while working as a bank loan officer at a new job, I received a shocking text message from my estranged husband, Ken. He had stolen my Audi SUV, using the extra set of keys that I had forgotten to take when I moved out of our house. Panic set in as I rushed to the parking garage to find my vehicle missing.

Travis and Jill had helped me move out recently but my emotions were still overwhelming me, and I had to take a moment in the ladies' room to gather myself before returning to work. It felt like the ground had been ripped out from under me, and I couldn't help but wonder what other nasty surprises Ken had in store for me during the divorce proceedings.

Belinda, a friend who I called to come pick me up, provided a much-needed sense of stability and support as I tried to navigate the tumultuous situation with Ken. Despite the challenges, I knew deep down that I had the strength to get through it and emerge on the other side.

As I sat at my desk, my mind raced with the contents of my stolen SUV. My cell phone charger, yoga bag, garage door opener, and my favorite Chanel sunglasses were all inside. Even my dad's original Monte Blanc pen and my work parking pass were in the cup holder. But why was I worried about these things when Ken had stolen my SUV? The anger within me grew stronger. How low could Ken sink? Did he sit around and think of ways to be hateful to me?

I immediately texted Ken, demanding the return of my SUV, but his response was that he had already sold it. He then demanded the engagement ring back, which had his family's diamonds. Despite it being my property, I agreed to return the ring, wanting nothing that reminded me of him. He was so narcissistic it was easier than the drama that would unfold if I didn't give in.

Ken's actions left me feeling tired and broken. He was a master manipulator who could lie with ease. It was shocking to see the vindictiveness of his revengeful behavior towards me, his wife of over a decade. My life was quickly falling apart as I faced cruelty and betrayal from the person I had shared a bed with every night. Anxiety enveloped me, and the bitter reality of the situation became a dreadful experience.

Nonetheless, I had to keep moving forward as Emma was depending on me. So, I decided to cash in my 401K and bought a used car that was several years old.

Going to work became a much-needed outlet for me as I was doing a good job and my self-esteem was beginning to return. However, one thing that bothered me was the anxiety that would envelop me whenever families with children came in. The small kids would often begin to whine or cry if their parent's business took too long, and I would feel a cloak of dread come over me. I was tired of always being scared, and could not understand where this anxiety and fear were coming from. Initially, I blamed it on Ken and the divorce, but I soon realized that it was something more significant.

During this time, I kept thinking about how worn out I was and how I hoped the anxiety would go away once the divorce was final. I struggled to breathe, and I wanted to feel safe again. I learned to minimize my problems and not complain, but to myself, I thought about how weary I was of always having to be on high alert and of being so afraid. I felt as if I could never lower my guard, and as a result, my weight was dropping, and I was getting thinner. It seemed I was just too nervous to eat.

My mother was unable to help me financially with the divorce, not that I would have asked her. After Dad died, she did the best she could to make a life on a limited income and live comfortably in Charleston with her sisters. She needed their emotional support, and I was glad she could not see me in this state.

I became skilled at presenting a facade of composure and assuring others that all was well with me. However, beneath the surface, I was shattered by the insidious presence of deceit, betrayal, and fear in my life. Even now, the thought sends shivers down my spine.

As a mother and wife, I have come to appreciate how easily women can lose themselves in the responsibilities of parenthood. It's astonishing how little time is devoted to self-care by mothers of young children. Despite this, I've managed to take charge of my life and provide my daughter Emma with a stable home. Emma and I share an unbreakable bond, which allows us to discuss anything, including sex. We've had numerous conversations about boys since it seemed like she was always being pursued. I recall telling her once that sperm can survive on a hard surface for up to five days, and she replied with, "Eww, Momma."

I despised the way people pitied me; it made me feel like I needed to console them. The forced conversations that began with "Hello, how are you doing?" were unbearable. I resented being the object of their sympathy.

Our lives are a tangled web of family secrets, blood ties, and parental influences that shape us, whether we like it or not. My life was no exception. Cobwebs of deception were exposed, and skeletons spilled out of the closet. My relationships suffered, causing me to withdraw from people for a time. My sister Jill was my confidant, and I don't know how I would have made it through without her and the grace of God.

Life is not a dress rehearsal, and for most people, there are no second chances to redo their life. However, I was fortunate enough to have a second chance when Logan, my adopted son, came into my life. He forever changed me, for better and for worse. Despite the challenges, I have landed on my feet and arrived at this place in life, and I suppose this is where I am supposed to be. Even after being lost during the dark years, I was able to recapture a lasting love and belong to a happy, smiling family. Unconditional love is so important, and I feel lucky to have it now.

"I love you," Emma texted.

"Love you more," I replied.

Memories flood over me at times. I don't mind the good ones, but the bad ones can really bring me down if I let them. The worst part is second-guessing the decisions I made then based on what I know now. I know it's irrational, but sometimes my mind just goes there.

My first husband, Ken, appeared to have everything a girl could want - he was tall, handsome, and polite. However, I later discovered that he was a master of disguise and extremely narcissistic. I cannot judge myself for the decisions I made before knowing the truth.

In recent years, I have learned that some of my supposed "friends" were only there for me during good times. As soon as things took a turn for the worse, they disappeared without a trace.

I have also realized that "truth" is subjective to some people, and the person I believed to be the most trustworthy was, in fact, the most dishonest. It's baffling.

Money can conceal all sorts of dirtiness, and image is often more important than wholeness. I have seen that family reputation can take precedence over integrity and character, and some people find it acceptable to resort to deceit to maintain that reputation.

Although I have moved on from that chapter in my life, I am still repulsed by some of the things I witnessed and heard. Much of my experience in that marriage was the antithesis of my dreams. Despite not being fresh in my mind, those memories have left an indelible mark on me. I grew in ways I never thought possible and did things that I never believed I would or should do.

Some of those days are entirely erased from my mind, or perhaps I have buried them so deep that they may never resurface. I prefer to believe they are gone, never to torment me again. However, amidst the turmoil, I still cherish the memories of warm, sunny, and beautiful days.

One of those days was when I first laid eyes on my precious Emma. She was like a little angel with perfect skin, delicate and soft, with tiny hands and feet. I had never seen a baby so beautiful. That day remains vivid in my mind and has never lost its brightness, even in the darkest of times.

Another vivid memory was when I walked into our newly built home for the first time. It was located in a gorgeous gated community with mature trees and stunning mountain views. The architect had delivered a floor plan that perfectly suited my taste, and the decorator chose fabrics, paint colors, and furnishings that made it feel like home.

As I was lost in thought, my phone rang, jolting me back to reality.

"Hey, Jax."

"My leg is starting to hurt, so I'm coming home to rest."

"Sure, the doctor said to take it easy for a few days."

"I'll be home soon. Love you."

"Love you more. Bye."

Jax had been playing golf and went into the woods to retrieve a ball. While searching, he disturbed a brown recluse spider nest and quickly retreated. Later, he noticed a red mark with two black spots on the back of his leg, right above his sock line, and went to see Dr. Keith.

"I called Dr. Keith, and he wants me to go to the hospital but I'm not going."

"Why would you do that?" I was upset, and my expression gave it away.

"Nugget, I'll be fine. Don't get all riled up."

I looked up brown recluse spider bites on Google and was horrified by the pictures of the venomous wound. The site indicated that sometimes it requires medical intervention to remove blackened, dead tissue. It also said the spider numbs you first, then puts his fangs in to inject you with poisonous venom. I knew people like that as well.

It has been reported that reactions to the venom of the bite can vary, with some individuals experiencing a delayed reaction, others an immediate reaction, and some having no reaction at all. For those who are sensitive to the venom, the bite site can develop into a volcano lesion, causing the damaged tissue to become gangrenous and leaving an open wound that can grow as large as a human hand.

"It's a very big deal, Jax, you need to take this seriously," I pleaded because I was scared.

"Dr. Keith took some blood for labs and I will go back when they are back," Jax replied.

However, that night while we were sleeping, Jax's condition worsened. He spiked a fever and was experiencing chills and nausea. "We need to go to the hospital now," I said urgently. No way I was losing him again.

But Jax refused, insisting that he needed to take a shower and pack his bag such as his camera, computer, and phone charger, so he could work from the hospital if necessary. Jax said he would go the next day if it was worse.

At that moment, anger engulfed my body, and I realized that this was my coping mechanism for dealing with fear. I had difficulty expressing any emotion, as I was emotionally closed off. I was in love with Jax and he was the most important man in my life!

Whenever I felt vulnerable, my past traumas would resurface, causing me to block out my feelings and pretend that everything was fine. Relearning how to feel my emotions was a challenging process, and I despised myself for allowing someone to attack me and pretending that everything was okay to maintain appearances.

Living with someone in the past who had unpredictable behavior had been difficult, as it made me feel out of control. It was a struggle to determine my own feelings and to stop using anger as my defense mechanism.

Whenever I felt anxious, disturbing images would flash through my mind, and I'd get the urge to flee. Fight or flight response was strong in me. To cope, I'd clench my jaw and tense my muscles. Unlike others, I didn't shut down when I faced discomfort - I got angry and pushed through any crisis, thanks to my traumatic past.

As Jax slept, I kept watch and waited for him to wake up. Jax was an independent man who had traveled to 38 countries to take photographs. He wasn't afraid of a spider bite. However, the next morning, red tracks were visible on his leg, and an infection had set in. Already on the phone with Jill, who had a nursing degree, we were discussing the situation. I thanked God for her expertise and urged Jax to go to the hospital immediately for IV antibiotics.

"Jax, it's time to go to the hospital. Do you want to be buried or cremated when you die?" I said jokingly.

"Don't worry, Kate. I'm not going to die. I'm not going to leave you. I'm fine," he replied.

"I am FINE too - Freaked out, Insecure, Neurotic, and Emotional," I retorted. "I may end up killing you before the spider bite does. Just look at your leg - the red tracks prove it's infected, and by the looks of it, your balls will drop off if you don't get to the hospital."

After Jax packed half of his belongings, we finally got into my car.

Jax was the ultimate man's man he was just a tough guy. As I drove towards the hospital, my car sputtered and jerked, and I realized we'd run out of gas. I put my head in my hands, knowing that Jax would say, "That's why I always fill up at a quarter of a tank."

A police car appeared behind us, and I jumped out and waved my arms frantically. The officer pulled up behind us, and I ran up to his window, explaining the situation. "We're on our way to the hospital and ran out of gas. Could you please take me to the station to buy a gas can and gas?" I said, holding up my white purse. "I have money with me."

The police officer nodded in agreement as I approached the squad car. I opened the front door, but before I could get in, he said, "Ma'am, you will need to get in the back." Embarrassed at my situation of running out of gas, I closed the front door and opened the back door, sliding into the hard plastic seat with a cage protecting the officer. It was my first time in a police car, and I was startled by the unfamiliar surroundings.

As we arrived at the gas station, I tried to open the back door to get out but failed several times. The officer chuckled and said, "Ma'am, you can't get out of the back of the car. You've never been in a cop car before, have you?" I sheepishly replied, "No."

He walked around to open the door for me and let me out. I returned with the full gas can in a flash, and we drove back to where Jax was still sitting in my car. Once again, I tried to open the door of the squad car and failed. The officer walked around to let me out and said, "Sorry." I thanked him for his help and we proceeded to the hospital.

Jill had already arranged a direct admission from Dr. Keith's office, and Jax was immediately put on IV antibiotics. The surgeon drained the abscess and cleaned out the necrotic tissue from Jax's leg. Luckily, the bloodwork came back okay, and he would be able to go home.

Jax has become one of the best and brightest things in my life since that dark and stressful time. When he arrived, I felt the tension drain away. Everything is so different now. I feel cherished, loved, valued, and special. In fact, it's becoming increasingly difficult to recall the sad, difficult times because so much good is happening now. My life has transformed, and I no longer feel abandoned. I'm now strong, bold, brave, and not timid or terrified. It's an entirely new life from what I had before.

However, I can't completely detach myself from the decade I spent with my first husband, Ken. Good or bad, each day of that time with him shaped me into the person I am today. I believe that a person is the sum total of all their experiences, and I see it in my life. Many things had to happen to overcome the odds thrown at me.

Growing up, I had a particular framework with which to view the world, and it was fine as long as I stayed within my element. But when I left my parents' home and ventured out on my own, my framework was put to the test, and its weak points were exposed. I didn't consider myself naive, but I wasn't streetwise either. I was just me.

CHAPTER 3

Growing up in our close-knit neighborhood, my sister Jill and I were surrounded by families who knew each other well. We all attended the same private prep school and were members of the Country Club of Asheville, which may not have been as exclusive as the Biltmore Country Club, but it was still our second home. After church on Sundays, the entire neighborhood would head over to the club to unwind and indulge in a large buffet lunch. It felt as though we were all part of one big extended family.

During the summers, our mothers would leave us in the care of the watchful black kitchen and dining room staff at the club. We spent our time participating in all of the club activities, including golf and tennis camps, as well as the swim team. On Saturdays, our dads played golf and would visit the men-only bar, the 19th Hole, which was located in the center of the club. Our favorite waitress, Dot, worked at the bar. Our parents loved her because she was strict and we always behaved when she was around. Dot always had our backs and treated every child with the same love and kindness. Every day, she would greet us with a warm embrace and a big ole booby hug. While we were allowed to sit inside and drink sweet tea, we were expected to be well-behaved and quiet in the dining room. However, we could let loose and have fun at the snack bar by the pool, since we were outside.

One event that stood out every fall was our high school homecoming dance. It was always a big deal, but I remember the year that Jax Harper asked me to be his date. I had been smitten with him since we first met at school, though he had no idea. Jax was the cutest guy in school, or at least I thought he was. Jax had an infectious smile, and twinkling blue eyes with a charming demeanor. He was about 5' 11", which was perfect for me since I was only 5' 3". He affectionately called me "Nugget," a nickname that stuck.

Mr. Harper drove us to dinner and to the homecoming dance that night since Jax didn't have his driver's license yet. First, he picked me up from my house, and we planned to have dinner at the country club before the dance. I was wearing a long red dress and a pair of my mom's high heels, which I had never walked in before, and felt a bit unsteady. When Jax arrived at my home, I stood at the top of the stairs waiting to make my grand entrance. Jill and Travis were already downstairs. Both Jax and my mom were standing at the foot of the stairs, while our black lab was curled up asleep on the landing. Carefully, I started down the stairs, but my heel caught in the hem of my long dress, causing me to lose my balance and tumble down the stairs, landing on the dog. The poor lab howled and ran away, while I jumped up, red- faced and embarrassed. Jax ran to me. "Nugget, Are you okay?" Laughing hysterically not wanting to appear flustered, I looked Jax right in the eyes and said, "I've been practicing that all day." He bent over and laughed heartily, putting his hands on his knees. Both heels on my mom's shoes had broken off, so she took me to her closet to find a pair of flats. It wasn't exactly the way I had envisioned starting my relationship with the boy who made my heart skip a beat.

I vividly recall the day when Jax first arrived at our school, having transferred from Texas. We were standing in the lunch line, and I was wearing my cheerleading uniform. Suddenly, I felt a hand lifting up my short skirt, exposing my tights which barely covered my behind. Unbeknownst to me, Jax had been observing the whole scene and he was incensed. He stormed over, snatched the guy's plastic lunch tray away, and then grabbed him by his letterman jacket, lifting him off the floor. Jax, who had spent his summer lifting hay bales at the ranch, warned him that if he ever tried anything like that again, he would have to answer to him. Jax admonished him, saying, "You don't treat young ladies like that." The guy looked stunned and quickly left the lunch line. Jax then introduced himself to me, flashing a dazzling megawatt smile. He said, "Jackson "Jax" Harper."

Roguishly handsome with fantastic biceps and a bit of an outsider since he was new. From that moment on, I couldn't help but feel a burning sense of infatuation for him.

Jax was not only incredibly good-looking, with his dark hair and piercing blue eyes that left you wanting more, but he was also hilarious and had impeccable timing. He was always cracking jokes and making me laugh. He was a Texas boy, and loved talking about ranching. Jax's family was extremely close, and they only moved to North Carolina because of his father's job, or so I thought at the time. Family was paramount for Jax, and I loved that about him.

Jax drove me in his pickup to a hillside underneath magnolia trees overlooking a field of yellow flowers. Jax was carrying his camera and began to take pictures of me. It was beautiful outside with a slight breeze blowing. Jax told me I looked pretty and I felt very close to him at that moment. We walked through the field of yellow flowers and I fell back into the yellow ocean laughing while Jax was taking my picture. Jax lay down beside me and we looked into the clouds. "Is that what you want to do, take pictures?" I asked.

"I want to be a photojournalist. Show people the beauty in the world that I see everywhere." Said Jax.

"That sounds so important, I just want to be a wife and mother, that's not really important," I said.

Jax got serious, "Of course it is. It's actually more important. Really. It's better to train children than repair men."

Why are you so great? I asked

"I was just thinking about being inseparable from you." Jax grinned.

He leaned in and put his arms around me and I closed my eyes as he kissed me.

Jax was quickly fitting into my life plan and comfortable with my family.

Jill and I were also brought up with a deep sense of family values. Our parents instilled in us the importance of family, and it was something that we both planned to carry on in our own lives. Our parents had always expected us to remain in the area after college, get married, and start families of our own. We both felt a strong sense of belonging that came from this closeness and it was something that provided us with a great deal of comfort.

Jax and I quickly became tight, and our bond grew stronger each day. He was a hugger and a hand-holder, and always called me, "Nugget," because he thought I was precious. Every moment of high school was filled with memories of Jax. Each morning, he would come and pick me up in his pick-up truck, and I would slide over to sit next to him. He would sing along to the songs on the radio, holding my hand and using it as a microphone before kissing the top of it. We even had a secret code to say "I love you" when we were too far apart to say it out loud. He would hold up three fingers, indicating "I love you," using his index finger for "I," the peace sign for "love," and the Boy Scout salute (three fingers) for "you." It was our little secret, and I only shared it with Jill, whom I trusted completely. Jax was my whole world.

Jax was always such a joy to be around. He had a way of making me laugh like no one else could, and being with him was always a good time. I'll never forget the way he used to wrap his arms around my waist and kiss the back of my hair. It all started one night at a bonfire when I was cold and he offered to be my human coat. When he kissed my hair, it sent shivers down my spine. We were so young and in love, and it felt like nothing could tear us apart.

We wrote each other notes and left them in each other's lockers at school. We were always together and never seemed to get sick of each other's company. Jax was always there for me when I needed someone to talk to, and he had a way of making me feel safe and protected. When we walked together, he would place his hand on the small of my back, which made me feel like he was looking out for me.

We dated all throughout high school, but after our senior year, Jax's father decided to move back to Texas to help run his grandfather's ranch. The patriarch was sick with cancer, and Jax's uncle couldn't handle everything on his own. That summer, I went to visit Jax in Texas, and it was the best time of my life. He called me his dream girl, and it felt like the perfect complement coming from him. Jax was all cowboy boots and country music, and he seemed to fit right in on the ranch. He was a natural at riding horses and was a skilled marksman. He was a good ranch hand and looked good in chaps.

The Harper's were a close-knit family and were careful about letting anyone get in.

Despite all of this, I knew that Jax loved me deeply, and I loved him just as much. But the distance between us was too great. His family was in Texas, and I knew that I couldn't ask him to leave the place he loved so much and be away from his family. When I boarded the plane to go back home, I knew that we would have to break up. We were going to colleges so far away. It was one of the hardest things I've ever had to do, but I knew that it was the right choice. Jax will always hold a special place in my heart, but I was not able to forget the love that we shared.

After a few weeks at home, I told Jax it was time to end things. "You need to be in Texas with your family. They need you there," I explained. "Your life is with them, just like mine is here in Asheville with my family."

Jax told me that he can't lose me and asked me to move to the ranch. He was very upset with me. He wanted to make it work.

That sad day is forever etched in my memory. We cried together on the phone, but I knew I had to put my family first, as my mother had taught me. I let Jax go, even though he promised to move back to North Carolina. I refused, not wanting to separate our families. We vowed to stay in touch and laughed through our tears. I always thought I'd find someone else, someone like Jax, but it never happened.

Jax studied journalism at Texas A&M during the week and worked at his family's ranch on the weekends. I always believed he chose that field because he knew how to tell a great story. Over time, he became a skilled photographer. We talked less and less while he was in college, eventually losing touch. But when we spoke on the phone, it felt like no time had passed. He still called me "Nugget." I often wondered what he was doing and how his family was.

Jax was the one who got away, but perhaps it was meant to be. God has a way of guiding us where we need to be. I was crushed when we split up. We were young and didn't realize how strong our connection was, how special. He owned my heart, but I rejected him because I couldn't handle that his family and the Lone Star State were his first loves. We both loved and were loyal to our families. I've compared every man I've met since to Jax, but none have measured up.

My self-esteem centered around being with people. I loved going for the big laugh, something Jax taught me. I wasn't stick thin like Jill, but blessed with curves, something I wasn't always comfortable with. My sense of humor helped me cover any insecurity I felt, especially during the years when I hid the chaos at home. Being popular was important, too. I wasn't overweight, just not as tall as Jill, but I had great hair, and I never let her forget it.

I had a knack for talking my way out of trouble. You know how it is – flash a quick smile or a coy look – and suddenly you're able to get away with just about anything. I remember one day when I was driving to school at UNC, I saw the flashing blue lights of a police car behind me. I pulled over and watched in the mirror as the officer approached my window, trying to think of the best way to talk my way out of a ticket.

When he asked for my license and registration, I flashed my most charming smile and pulled my shoulders back, feeling grateful for my curves. I dripped with Southern charm and pleaded with him to let me off with just a warning. Much to my relief, the officer seemed to be receptive to my charms and even chuckled at my efforts.

But just as I thought I had successfully sweet-talked my way out of trouble, the officer told me to look inside the squad car. "Do you see that man?" he asked, pointing to a stern-looking figure in the passenger seat. "He's my sergeant, and he'll kick my butt if I don't give you a ticket."

Feeling a little deflated but not willing to give up just yet, I said, "Well, my Dad's going to kick my ass if you do." The officer burst out laughing at my response and shook his head in amusement. After a moment's hesitation, he decided to let me off with just a warning ticket, much to my relief.

That experience taught me that sometimes, even the best of charms and Southern hospitality can only get you so far. But it also reminded me of the importance of being quick on my feet and always having a clever response ready, no matter what situation I found myself in.

CHAPTER 4

College was an exciting time for me, and attending the University of North Carolina provided the convenience of being close to home. Jill had started there a year earlier, so she acted as my guide and mentor. We decided to join the same sorority, becoming ΣAE (Sigma Alpha Epsilon) little sisters. This fraternity had a long-standing history, established in 1856 at the University of Alabama as the first national fraternity in the Deep South. In my first semester, I resided on campus in a dormitory, but later Jill and I moved into an apartment, enjoying the freedom and independence it offered. Balancing our studies with having fun became a priority throughout our college years.

One memorable event was the ΣAE's Halloween frat costume party. Jill found a beautiful angel costume and borrowed a devil costume adorned with shimmering red sequins and accompanied by a matching red pitchfork. I loved the fiery red dress, so I embraced my role as the devil, while Jill embodied the innocence of an angel. Travis showed up in a Viking costume and Jill shook her head. Travis walked over and asked for beer from the guy working the keg.

Amidst the anticipation and preparations for the party, I realized I had forgotten to eat anything before leaving. Meeting up with another group at the Alpha Gam house, we made our way to the party together. Our arrival elicited giggles from fellow party-goers as they saw Jill and me, dressed in contrasting angel and devil costumes. Everyone was vying to win the costume contest, and I remember a standout costume—a girl cleverly dressed as a "brick house" accompanied by a guy who humorously depicted a "cereal killer," sporting miniature cereal boxes affixed to his shirt. It was a lighthearted and entertaining evening.

Inside the party, the music blared loudly, and the space was crowded with enthusiastic attendees. Each of us was handed a red Solo cup filled with a concoction known as "hunch punch." This potent mix contained pure grain alcohol and was prepared in a large garbage can situated next to a keg of beer. To this day, I'm uncertain about the origins of its name, but it might have been due to the fact that the drink often led to hunching over in discomfort or the aftermath of a terrible hangover. Regardless, the girls opted for the red punch while the guys stuck to beer, and together we danced energetically to the music, reveling in the spirited atmosphere.

During the course of the evening, I was introduced to various people, including Ken Burnett, who hailed from Asheville like me. The Burnetts were a prominent family in the area, known for their wealth and influence. Their prosperity derived from the grandfather, who had amassed fortunes through timber investments and land speculation. Everyone in Asheville was well aware of the Burnetts, but at UNC, Ken seemed to hold sway over the social scene. He had previously flunked out of Clemson due to his preference for partying over attending classes. Being a few years older than me, Ken had returned to school after taking a hiatus. Given his family's affluence, he seemed more interested in enjoying his time at college than in pursuing graduation. I suspected his coursework primarily revolved around the art of spending money, or perhaps he simply enrolled in whichever courses the financially privileged managed to pass.

The effects of the alcohol in the punch hit me swiftly, and I found myself instantly buzzed. It was well past midnight, and the party was in full swing when I playfully prodded Ken with my pitchfork, asking if he wanted to accompany me to hell. Jill couldn't help but laugh and quipped, "Whoa! Satan called and wants his pitchfork back."

Recognizing my inebriated state, Jill decided it was best for me to return to the apartment. She understood that the combination of the red dress, the crowded atmosphere, and the alcohol was a recipe for disaster. Ken, being friendly and already acquainted with everyone, offered to drive Jill and the "devil girl" home. Jill agreed, and with Travis and Ken's assistance, I got into his car, unwittingly setting in motion a chain of events that would significantly impact my life. Little did I know at the time the magnitude of that decision.

Upon arriving at our apartment, Ken helped Jill get me inside and then smartly ordered a pizza. He stuck around, engaging in easy conversation, and we all sat together, sipping coke, indulging in pizza, and sharing laughter over the night's costumes. Ken had dressed up as the Mad Hatter from Alice in Wonderland and looked hilariously comical. Travis was asleep on the couch.

Following that night, Ken and I began hanging out more frequently, often in the company of our mutual friends Mark and Maggie, as well as Jill and Travis. We had a great time going out for meals and catching movies—a typical college experience filled with leisure and the pursuit of enjoyment. Group outings became commonplace, especially when the financially privileged among us were generously covering the expenses.

Ken's luxurious car became a regular mode of transportation, and he took pleasure in chauffeuring me around and lavishing me with his financial resources. He relished his status as a prominent figure on campus. Tall, tanned, with a brilliant smile and reddish- brown hair, Ken seemed to know everyone wherever we went. He possessed a sociable nature and always took the initiative in planning various activities. Yet, he was also acutely aware of his image and deeply concerned about what others thought of him.

Jill informed me that Ken had developed feelings for me, but I didn't share the same level of interest. His wealthy background and striking appearance made other girls believe I was foolish not to pursue a relationship with him. While I found him occasionally goofy, I recognized it as just part of his personality. He was undeniably likable, and we started off as friends, gradually growing closer over the course of the school year. Ken was always making plans, and I often went along with them. Ken was always a gentleman and never tried anything.

As our bond strengthened, Ken opened up to me about his family and the pressures he faced to meet their expectations. He divulged that he confided in his mother, Maureen Burnett, about everything that transpired in his life. When summer arrived, and we all returned to our respective homes to live with our parents, I learned that Maureen, Ken's mother, wasn't pleased with his new girlfriend. However, it seemed that she didn't particularly approve of any girl Ken brought home.

Jill accompanied Ken and me as we drove up to the Burnett estate. Upon entering, we found Ken's parents, Maureen and Forrest, engaged in conversation with his brother, Robert. Ken described Robert as the epitome of the perfect son. Given Forrest's favoritism towards Robert, Maureen was fiercely protective of Ken.

The kitchen was expansive, adorned with cold granite surfaces. I could sense Maureen's icy stare as she scrutinized me from head to toe. While she knew everything about me, I knew very little about her. The introductions were formal, and soon Forrest and Robert excused themselves to indulge in a round of golf. Ken, less interested in sports compared to his brother, prioritized his appearance and fashion sense. He possessed the looks, while Robert was the athletic one.

Maureen treated me with a chilling indifference, speaking to me curtly. I couldn't help but wonder what I had done to offend her. She was obviously an unhappy person. Nonetheless, my upbringing in the South compelled me to engage in small talk. Eventually, Ken led me outside to explore the backyard, leaving Jill behind in the kitchen. Maureen seized the opportunity to corner Jill and inquire about our relationship. It was an uncomfortable experience for Jill, and she was visibly upset when I returned inside. After changing his clothes, Ken and I departed for the evening.

Later, when Jill and I returned home, she recounted the conversation with Maureen. "That woman is mean and cold. She genuinely questions if you're good enough for Ken," Jill expressed. When I inquired about the specifics of what Maureen had said, Jill explained that it was not so much the content but rather the cold and dismissive manner in which she spoke.

The summer proved to be busy, with Jill and I planning to work at our fathers' law office. Meanwhile, Ken's family embarked on their annual beach vacation. I suspect Maureen was secretly pleased by our temporary separation, as our relationship began to cool.

During that summer, I received a call from Jax, who invited me to spend a few weeks at the ranch. Eager for a job change, and excited to see Jax and a break from the law firm, I gladly accepted the offer. Jax mentioned that his uncle could provide me with employment ordering supplies for the ranch, a position that paid more than I was accustomed to, and I would have accommodations in the guest house. I quickly booked my flight, excited for the upcoming adventure.

As soon as I arrived at the ranch, our relationship picked up right where it left off. I ended up extending my stay, and our romance reignited. Being with Jax was everything I had ever wanted, and that summer became a perfect whirlwind of love and excitement. Ken never really did it for me and Jax was a joy to be around. He took me to Duke's, a country music bar where we could dance the night away with line dancing. We frequented the place and had a blast two-stepping together. To complete my ensemble, Jax recognized that I needed Wrangler jeans and a pair of cowboy boots, so he bought them for me. My new boots had a touch of sparkle and a hint of red trim, perfectly fitting my personal style.

While staying at the ranch, an unfortunate event occurred—Jax's great-aunt passed away. As per the family's tradition, someone needed to stay home to receive the food brought by relatives and friends. I volunteered for the task, but after a few hours, boredom got the best of me, and curiosity led me to explore the off-limits upstairs area. Against better judgment, I ventured into the master suite.

In the closet, I discovered a peculiar sight. On the top shelf were several white foam heads adorned with wigs. It struck me as odd because I had never seen Jax's aunt wearing a wig. Furthermore, I noticed size ten pumps and a collection of dresses in size fourteen. Given that Jax's aunt was petite, it was evident that those items did not belong to her. Suddenly, it dawned on me— the woman I occasionally glimpsed in the upstairs window after dinner was, in fact, Jax's uncle dressed in women's clothing. It seemed to be the family's well-kept secret. The revelation left me in shock since I was naive.

Suddenly, I heard a creaking floorboard, and panic washed over me. I turned around to leave, only to find Jax's uncle standing in the doorway. My face flushed with embarrassment as he reminded me that no one was allowed in that room. I lowered my head and hastily made my exit, my heart racing.

The next time Jax and I had a chance to talk privately, I mustered up the courage to inquire about his uncle. Jax and his brothers were taken aback and felt deeply uncomfortable with the situation. Jax also shared that the real reason their family moved from Texas to North Carolina was this. His father relocated the family to Asheville, and then eventually moved back to Texas due to Jax's grandfather's illness. It was a secret for the family, and Jax preferred not to discuss it extensively. His uncle's behavior was just one of those skeletons they kept hidden.

The following day, I received a phone call from my mom, and the tone of her voice conveyed grave news. She informed me that my father had suffered a severe heart attack, urging me to fly home immediately. Daddy's condition was critical, and time was of the essence. Jill had already booked my ticket, so Jax assisted me in packing and drove me to the airport promptly.

The airport farewell with Jax was hurried and filled with emotion. In the midst of the bustling crowd, there was no time for proper goodbyes. However, as I glanced back, I caught Jax flashing his fingers, counting 1, 2, 3—a silent expression of his love for me.

The flight back home was a blur as I wrestled with overwhelming emotions. Waves of guilt crashed over me, regretting my decision to be away from my father's office that summer. I had yearned to be with Jax in Texas, and now I found myself questioning my choices. If only I had known what was going to happen… but how could I have known? Trying to rationalize my actions only intensified my self-blame.

Jill met me at the airport, and without delay, we hurried to Mission Hospital where Daddy was admitted. Anxious and uncertain, I hesitated to enter the room, not knowing what to expect. Jill tried to prepare me, saying that Daddy was unresponsive, but nothing could have prepared me for what I was about to see.

As I walked into the room, leading the way with Jill following, I was taken aback. The person lying on the bed didn't resemble my Daddy. He lay motionless, connected to tubes, his face pale and drawn, his eyes closed. Dark circles accentuated the exhaustion and a breathing tube was inserted into his mouth. Overwhelmed, I felt a wave of dizziness, grabbing onto the foot of the bed to steady myself. How could this be happening?

Mom appeared exhausted, every ounce of strength drained from her. She rushed to help me regain my balance, then enveloped me in her arms, sobbing from the depths of her being. As her daughter, I had never witnessed her so frightened and worn out. Jill quickly stepped into the role of a big sister, helping both Mom and me regain composure. Standing in the middle of the room, all I wanted was to escape to a safe place, but there was nowhere to go.

Daddy's condition stabilized, but he never regained consciousness. The widow maker is what the nurse said when describing the part of the heart that was affected. After spending ten days in the hospital, he was transferred to a care facility where he could receive continuous monitoring.

Despite my impending senior year of college, I knew that Mom needed me at home. Thankfully, UNC Asheville had implemented a new program allowing remote learning. I could register for classes, watch lectures on line, and submit homework by email. Once a week, I had to visit the campus for consultations or quizzes with teachers, but I could study from home and complete my final year while assisting Mom.

Meanwhile, Jax returned to Texas A&M to complete his degree in photojournalism. The stress of my father's illness and my sudden departure took its toll on our relationship. Jax was supportive of my decision to move back home, but time slipped away quickly, and the demands of life caused us to drift apart.

Daddy passed away nearly three months to the day after having the heart attack. Mom nearly fell to pieces. Looking back, I am grateful that I moved back in with her to help during this terrible, tragic time. For some reason, I was able to come to terms with Daddy's condition much easier than Mom was. Perhaps it was because I felt a tremendous responsibility to be there for her during this period. Throughout it all, Mom and I grew extremely close and found solace in sharing our thoughts and emotions.

One day, a package arrived from Jax. Opening it, I discovered a note alongside the cowboy boots he had bought for me. My hands trembled as I unfolded the paper to read his words.

"Nugget,

Thank you for the wonderful summer. It meant the world to me being with you. It was an incredibly special time with my dream girl. I am deeply sorry about your dad and want you to be there for your momma and Jill. I am glad we had that time together, but you need to stay in Asheville.

I love you.

Jax"

Now it was my turn to be consumed by wrenching sobs from deep within. I knew that Jax was right, but that realization didn't ease the pain in my heart. My love for him was so profound that it defied explanation. I felt as though my life was spiraling out of control—first Daddy, and now this. How much more could I endure and still maintain my sanity? I kept it in, and tried to be strong. But what I really wanted was to be held by the two people's arms that were no longer there—who would never hold me again. I cried a month's worth of tears that day.

CHAPTER 5

"Hello," I said, taking the phone from my purse and preparing myself for the conversation ahead.

"Hi, Kate. This is Ken. What have you been up to?" His voice on the other end of the line brought a rush of memories flooding back. It felt like a lifetime since we had last spoken, and so much had transpired since then.

We spent nearly an hour catching up on the latest news about our friends and family. Ken seemed genuinely saddened when I told him about Daddy's passing. I chose not to mention Jax—the pain from that chapter of my life was still raw. Nevertheless, hearing Ken's voice was comforting amidst everything I had been through. After feeling so down for so long, Ken was a fresh breath of air. He was a familiar friend. Jill told me it was obvious Ken liked me. Everyone said I was crazy for not going for it, but you know while he was perfect for me on paper, the same spark was not there that had been with Jax. Still, Ken wooed me, and slowly like everyone else I eventually started to fall under his spell.

When Daddy passed away, Jill and I leaned on each other for support during the funeral. We each had a unique relationship with him. As the oldest, Jill connected with Daddy in a practical and almost business-like manner. Her logical-minded approach enabled her to understand and relate to Daddy's profession as a lawyer. My sister was my anchor, always there to help me stay afloat.

Daddy was a kind-hearted man who never wanted his girls to feel any pain, but he also taught us to be strong. I remember when I was about three years old and found my red beta fish dead in its bowl. I ran to Daddy, crying inconsolably. He reassured me that the veterinarian could fix the fish, so we hurriedly took it to the clinic. When we entered the exam room, the vet took the fish and returned with it swimming happily in the bowl. I clapped my hands in delight. Only as an adult did I learn that Daddy had called ahead and asked the vet's office to run next door to the pet store and buy a replacement fish. The vet was a close friend of Daddy's, and they played golf together. This story always touched my heart and taught me the importance of protecting the ones you love. Daddy often said that in life, you need something to do, someone to love, and something to look forward to. His wisdom and unwavering love helped me find stability even in the midst of life's storms.

We loved sharing stories about Daddy, particularly those moments when he was running late and doing funny things. Like the time he placed his briefcase and a banana on the roof of his Mercedes and drove off. When Jill and I left for school that morning, we discovered the briefcase in the driveway and the banana in the street. Another time, he absentmindedly placed his coffee in the car door cup holder and slammed the door shut, splattering coffee all over his shirt and tie. Jill and I were enjoying our breakfast when he returned to change his clothes. Mom just shook her head, knowing how much Daddy needed her grounding presence.

But perhaps the best story happened one morning when he thought he was home alone. After taking his shower, he walked naked toward the kitchen to grab some coffee. Unbeknownst to him, Georgia, our housekeeper, was standing at the glass door about to come inside. When Daddy spotted her, he panicked and started running, only to slip on the wooden floor and hit his forehead on the doorway leading into the dining room. He fell to his knees, blood dripping from his head, with his rear end sticking up in the air. Georgia witnessed the entire spectacle and rushed after him, screaming, "Mr. Stenson! Are you okay?" Jill still bursts into laughter whenever we reminisce about Georgia seeing Daddy in such an awkward situation.

These stories served as a reminder of the joy and laughter Daddy brought into our lives. They were cherished memories that helped us cope with his absence. As the days turned into weeks, Jill and I continued to support one another, finding solace in our shared experiences and the love our father had instilled in us.

Little did I know, unexpected connections and new beginnings were waiting just around the corner.

After Daddy passed, Mom went through a tough time, and Jill and I did our best to help her navigate the waves of grief, anger, and despair. We were surprised by the depth of Mom's anger, but she confided in us one day, expressing how unfair Daddy's death felt. He had been full of life, healthy and strong, and the stroke that took him seemed like a cruel and calculated blow.

I decided to study law and Jill studied education. And Travis, well Travis studied partying. That summer Travis proposed and his family pitched in so they could be married at the country club.

Jill's engagement to Travis brought a shift in Mom's focus. True to Jill's dreams, the wedding was a grand southern affair, set beneath the blossoming branches of a magnolia tree. It was a beautiful ceremony, and Mom poured her energy into making it a special day. We all felt a tinge of sadness, though, knowing that Daddy couldn't be there to give his little girls away. He had always joked about protecting us, even playfully threatening Travis with a shotgun shell if he ever made Jill cry. We knew those jokes carried a hint of truth. Daddy's absence weighed heavily on Jill and me, and we shared silent tears for the father who couldn't witness our weddings.

Seeing Jill get married reignited my own dreams of finding love and getting married. Though my heart still ached for Jax, I knew it was time to move forward. I decided to join a singles networking group and started attending their monthly social events in hopes of meeting someone new and intriguing.

The following week, my friend Maggie and I attended one of these social gatherings. We mingled with a large group of twenty- something singles, observing their interactions and silently noting what to avoid in the dating scene. Amidst the crowd, I was caught off guard when I bumped into Ken in the hallway after leaving the ladies' room. Ken warmly embraced me, his sharp attire and charming demeanor as captivating as ever. We struck up a conversation, and I discovered that he was currently working in his family's timber business but found himself utterly bored.

As Ken and I sat at a table, engrossed in conversation, an unfamiliar man approached from behind and placed his hands on my shoulders. His arrogant demeanor was evident as he rudely interrupted our discussion. Fed up with his behavior, I couldn't contain my frustration any longer and firmly told him to remove his hands. "Don't touch me," I asserted. The man responded by making snide comments about my supposed unfriendliness and the need for me to be more considerate. Enraged by his audacity, I made it clear that he was the last person I would ever entertain the thought of being with, and any interaction would be solely to ensure I stayed far away from him.

Ken laughed so hard that I thought he was going to start crying. He was accompanied by his friend, Mark. When he asked Maggie and me if we would be willing to leave the social gathering and go to a movie instead. Ready for a change of scenery, the four of us agreed and headed to the cinema. Afterward, we decided to continue the evening at a bar, enjoying drinks and listening to music.

That night with Ken marked a rekindling of our dating relationship, and we began to spend more time together. Ken made a point to call me every day and frequently visited me. He assured me that his parents would not interfere as they had done in the past, emphasizing his independence. However, his mother, Maureen, held unfounded fears that I might try to trap him by getting pregnant, and she instilled in him the notion that I was solely interested in his wealth. While it was true that I enjoyed the perks of dating a wealthy individual, there were deeper aspects that kept me connected to Ken. As our friendship blossomed, our relationship grew in unexpected ways.

Ken and I often engaged in double-dates with Mark and Maggie, adding an extra layer of enjoyment to our outings. The four of us frequently dined out, attended movies, concerts, and visited the beach whenever we could escape from work. Given my financial situation and recent move to a new apartment, Ken's generosity in paying for our meals provided much-needed support.

Ken's outgoing nature and penchant for socializing naturally led him to take charge of planning our activities. He assumed the role of the "event planner" for our group, organizing our weekends and having a knack for remembering people's names. He would occasionally drop a name or two during our gatherings, impressing others and sometimes gaining special favors.

One of our favorite pastimes was spending time downtown during Belle Cher, Asheville's Mardi Gras celebration. The festival exuded a vibrant and carefree atmosphere, as we joyously danced in the streets until the police ushered us away. Belle Cher's unique blend of people, ranging from street performers to members of the country club, created an eclectic mix where everyone danced to their own beat.

Amidst the revelry, we also had to remain vigilant and mindful of our surroundings. Mark, in particular, had a tendency to become excessively intoxicated on occasion. During one evening of the festival, he momentarily stepped aside to indulge in a shot of Jagger and narrowly escaped a confrontation with two individuals looking for a fight. Recognizing the escalating situation, we decided it was best to leave to avoid any altercations. The last thing we wanted was for Mark to end up in trouble with the police.

During the winter holiday season, our family decided to embark on a snow skiing trip to foster reconnection after our father's passing. We all flew to Lake Tahoe and stayed at a ski-in/ski-out lodge. The moment we arrived, we were greeted by a picturesque snowy landscape, with fresh powder covering the surroundings. It was said to be the best snowfall Lake Tahoe had witnessed in three years. Jill and Travis took the lead and ventured down the slopes on the first day, with the rest of us following suit. It turned out to be a perfect day of skiing, fostering both enjoyment and a sense of togetherness among us.

On the second day, my mom and aunts decided to stay cozy in the lodge, indulging in hot schnapps by the crackling fire and sharing cherished family stories. Laughter and tears intertwined as the day progressed, providing a much-needed release for them after the stress and tension surrounding my father's passing. By five o'clock, they were more than a little tipsy, so we guided them off to bed for a couple of hours before dinner. Later, my mom confided in me that those moments with her sisters allowed her to finally let go of the weight she had been carrying since my father's departure.

Day three greeted us with even colder temperatures and a brisk wind. Snowboarders dotted the landscape, effortlessly soaring over moguls and hills as we ascended on the ski lift. When we reached the top, Travis wasted no time and zoomed down the mountain, closely followed by Jill. Not seeing Jill pass by, I decided to pause and turn back, seeking her whereabouts. Suddenly, everything went dark. The next fragment of memory I have is lying on the snow, surrounded by people shouting, and a warm sensation emanating from my head.

Someone had alerted the Ski Patrol, and help was on its way. When I inquired about what had happened, Jill explained that a snowboarder had leaped off an embankment and collided with me, striking my head with his board. The injury proved severe enough that I had to be transported to the hospital by ambulance. Jill accompanied me, her worry palpable throughout the journey to the emergency room. My head throbbed relentlessly, my hair drenched in blood, and my neck numb. To ensure no further harm, the doctors fitted me with a halo device to stabilize my head. Amidst the pain and confusion, I couldn't help but wonder if my red lipstick had managed to withstand the ordeal, a trivial thought amidst the circumstances.

For several days, I remained in a medically induced coma, my awakening met by the sight of Ken sitting attentively in a chair by my hospital bed. Startled, I questioned why he was there. He explained that as soon as Maggie informed him of the accident, he rushed to be by my side. Ken had brought flowers and a card to brighten the hospital room and uplift my spirits.

Throughout the entirety of my two-week stay in the hospital, Ken never left my side. He provided companionship and support as my head and neck slowly healed. The impact from the snowboard had resulted in a cracked cervical vertebra, prompting the doctors to exercise utmost caution in preventing further harm. When my family returned to Asheville after a week, Ken assured them that he would stay with me. My mom needed to attend to matters back home, and both Travis and Jill had work commitments.

Ken made sure to highlight his family's wealth to the hospital staff. For him, prestige and social status were instrumental in the pursuit of a fulfilling life. As my suitor and protector, he relished the special treatment he received from the nurses and doctors due to his association with wealth and influence.

During my time in the hospital, as Ken tirelessly attended to my needs, a newfound appreciation for his thoughtfulness and dedication blossomed within me. His extravagant gestures and lavish gifts showcased his ability to create a spectacle. Unbeknownst to me, I found myself falling in love, relishing the attention and care that Ken showered upon me. His unwavering commitment to being by my side and forsaking other obligations spoke volumes about his feelings for me and the depth of our relationship.

As the days passed, the nurses became familiar with Ken, thanks to his daily offerings of donuts to bribe them each morning. It seemed to create a positive rapport, and I received exceptional care from them. It was cute. I was starting to fall for Ken. When the time came for me to leave the hospital, Ken accompanied me on the flight from Lake Tahoe, adamant about upgrading our tickets to first class.

Back at home, after the accident, Ken and I became inseparable, making the most of our free time by engaging in various activities together. He took pleasure in showering me with extravagant gifts, much to the envy of my friends. I, however, reveled in the luxurious attention. My family, too, held a favorable opinion of Ken, deeming him a suitable future husband for me. His position as my closest confidant held great significance, particularly for my mother, who yearned for nothing but the best for her daughter.

As time went on, it became increasingly evident that Ken was likely to propose, but the question lingered: when would it happen? Hope welled up within me, anticipation building, as I eagerly awaited the next chapter of our relationship…

CHAPTER 6

Ken's family had a tradition of spending a week at Myrtle Beach every summer. Their chosen retreat was the Marina Inn at Grande Dunes, a luxurious establishment that satisfied Maureen's insistence on top-notch accommodations. It was the first time I had been invited to join them, and I was thrilled to discover that I had a room all to myself. Maureen had made it clear that Ken and I should have separate rooms since we weren't married. The same went for Ken's brother, Robert, and his wife, who had their own private space. The rest of the extended family, including aunts, uncles, and cousins, each had their designated quarters as well.

Aunt Evie, a force to be reckoned with in the Burnett family, was a regular on these vacations. She took charge of organizing dinner reservations and outings, and she made sure everyone knew about it. Aunt Evie had a strong personality and was considered the matriarch of the family. She carried herself with a dignified air, reflecting her deep-rooted Southern heritage. Always dressed to the nines in designer clothing, complete with matching accessories from high-end stores, she had an air of refinement that couldn't be ignored. And when Aunt Evie looked down her nose at you over her reading glasses, you knew not to cross her. Her sharp wit, coupled with a sarcastic sense of humor, often caught people off guard. She had a way of saying what others were only thinking. It was clear that Aunt Evie held significant sway in the family and within the wider Asheville community.

Despite Maureen's best efforts, Aunt Evie never warmed up to her. Even though Maureen would put on a show to impress her, Aunt Evie saw right through it. To Aunt Evie, Maureen was simply someone who married into money, a fact she never hesitated to point out whenever the opportunity arose. She valued bloodline and heritage, and in her eyes, Maureen did not meet the criteria of being "of the blood."

During the vacation, the atmosphere was rife with competition. Ken was always trying to outdo his brother and gain the favor and attention of both Aunt Evie and his father, Forrest. It became an exhausting ordeal, as I felt like I was constantly under scrutiny by the family. Their relentless questioning made me wonder if I needed a security clearance to be part of their inner circle. However, being naturally competitive, I was determined not to be overshadowed and was ready to hold my own in this high-stakes family dynamic.

My family was not poor, and they had raised me with proper values. However, in Maureen's eyes, I still fell short of being suitable for Ken. Despite the amount of time I had spent with the family, she seemed even more distant and cold towards me on this trip. It was disheartening, and I tried my best to avoid any unnecessary conflicts with her. The tension was palpable, and I felt constant pressure to prove myself worthy of Ken and his family's approval.

Late one afternoon, as the sun began to set, Ken suggested taking a walk along the beach. We were already dressed for dinner, but I happily agreed. Holding hands, we strolled along the shoreline, enjoying the warm breeze and the sound of crashing waves. As we walked, I noticed that Ken's hands were unusually cold, but I dismissed it as a minor curiosity.

To my surprise, we came across a magnificent sandcastle standing proudly in the sand. As we approached, I noticed something hanging over the entrance—an elegant black scarf with a glistening object tied to it. As we got closer, I gasped in amazement. It was an engagement ring! My heart raced, and my breath caught in my throat as Ken knelt down on one knee, taking my hand in his. With a look of pure love in his eyes, he asked those four words that would change our lives forever, "Kate, will you make me the happiest man ever and marry me?"

Time seemed to stand still in that moment, and the weight of the world rested on my answer. Wanting to maintain an air of poise and composure, I managed to whisper a heartfelt

"Yes." Ken's face lit up with joy as he rose to his feet and embraced me tightly. Then, he delicately slipped the ring onto my finger—a dazzling two-carat princess-cut diamond adorned with two exquisite round diamonds on each side.

It was later revealed that the scarf Ken used for the proposal was the same one Forrest had used when he proposed to Maureen years ago. He had carefully threaded the ring through the scarf, creating a beautiful presentation. The Burnett family placed great importance on the engagement story, and I was honored to be a part of their tradition.

Ken's parents had even hired a security guard to ensure the ring's safety during our walk on the beach. As soon as Ken had proposed, the guard approached us to offer his congratulations before discreetly stepping away. Unbeknownst to me, the entire Burnett family had been discreetly watching the proposal from a nearby dock, dressed in matching outfits. After the magical moment, they joined us at the sandcastle, and a professional photographer captured the joyous occasion.

Overwhelmed with happiness, I was completely taken by surprise. It was a moment of pure bliss, receiving the keys to this castle of love. Little did I know, there were still unexpected challenges lurking within the castle's walls, waiting to reveal themselves.

Maureen wasted no time informing me that the diamonds on the sides of my engagement ring were from her earrings. She declared that the ring had now become a cherished heirloom, destined to stay within the family and be passed down through generations. I was taken aback by her sudden talk of babies and the future, especially since I hadn't even had the chance to share the news of our engagement with my own family.

Needing a moment of tranquility, I gently pulled away from the bustling crowd and shifted my gaze toward the serene beauty of the Grande Dunes. The sunlight played upon the water, creating a mesmerizing dance of sparkling reflections that momentarily eased my racing thoughts. But as the sun began its descent, casting hues of gold and orange across the sky, I knew it was time to join the others for dinner.

That night, conversations revolved solely around the wedding— the date, the venue, and every minute detail. Aunt Evie, true to form, adamantly stated that the wedding would take place at the country club. Maureen chimed in, seemingly determined to provoke a reaction, insisting that the venue should be wherever my mother desired. She knew well that such a statement would ruffle Aunt Evie's feathers. It was a stark reminder that the wedding preparations were just the beginning of the drama that awaited us. Once again, I couldn't shake off the feeling of being an outsider, struggling to find my place amidst the mounting tensions.

The wedding planning quickly descended into a frenzy, resembling a tumultuous college hazing rather than a joyous celebration. Everyone, from the assertive women in the family to Ken himself, had strong opinions and desires. However, it was Aunt Evie who held the reins of authority, refusing to accept any objections or compromises. She was a force to be reckoned with, relentless in her pursuit of control.

The first clash emerged over the wedding invitations. Aunt Evie and Ken staunchly insisted on engraved invitations, dismissing the idea of printed ones. Personally, I had no strong preference, so I decided to have two sets made—one engraved for the Burnett family and friends, and the other printed for my own loved ones. Adding to the chaos, Maureen demanded that all the RSVPs be sent to her house so she could meticulously track each response. With the growing presence of control freaks within the Burnett clan, I couldn't help but question whose wedding it truly was.

To my surprise, Forrest made a peculiar request—he wanted their family name to be included on the invitation, positioned just below my family's name. This request struck me as odd, considering they weren't contributing financially to the wedding. Firmly, I refused to comply, much to Forrest's discontent. It baffled me why he would insist on having his name on his own son's wedding invitation; it simply felt out of place. As if that wasn't enough, Forrest also expressed dissatisfaction with the newspaper announcement about the wedding, as his first and middle names had been inadvertently switched.

During a lunch outing with Jill, she finally disclosed something that had been weighing on her since our initial meeting. While delicately savoring our salads, she revealed that Maureen had confided in her, claiming that I wasn't good enough for Ken. The revelation shook me to the core. Although I had sensed Maureen's lack of warmth towards me, I never imagined she held such a low opinion of my worthiness. Jill expressed her desire to confront Maureen, suggesting that perhaps it was Ken who fell short of deserving me.

The newfound knowledge cast a shadow of doubt over my happiness, leaving me feeling uncertain and vulnerable as I navigated the complexities of my relationship with Ken and the challenges presented by the Burnett family.

Ken possessed an undeniable charm that made it hard not to be drawn to him. He had a knack for walking that fine line between showing off and ingratiating himself to others. Kate and I often teased him, saying he could win an Oscar for his charismatic performances. During one of our conversations, Jill brought up Jax and wondered how he would react to the news of our impending marriage. I brushed it off, noting that Jax was always off on his international photography adventures, so he probably hadn't heard yet.

To spare my dear mother from the overwhelming stress of the Burnett family's wedding planning, I shielded her from the intricate details and allowed them to take the reins. It seemed like everyone in that family had an opinion and was determined to assert it. Fortunately, Mom started spending more time with her sisters in Charleston, distancing herself from the chaos that consumed Asheville.

The choice of flowers became yet another point of contention. I had initially wanted elegant white roses for the bouquets, but considering the potential cost, I decided to include gardenias, thinking it would bring the price down. To my surprise, it had the opposite effect—the price doubled! When the florist contacted Maureen about the change, she erupted in fury, demanding to know what I had done. Feeling the need to pacify the situation, I promptly called and reverted back to the all-rose arrangement. This only fueled Maureen's anger toward me, and she swiftly reverted it back to her preference. Wanting to maintain peace and harmony, I went along with her decision. After all, it was Jill who had envisioned the fairy tale wedding, not me. I would have been content with beautiful photographs, a simple ceremony, and straight to the honeymoon!

Ken had chosen six groomsmen, while I had an equal number of bridesmaids—a lively and enjoyable group of friends. I opted for stunning red bridesmaid dresses from New York, and they looked absolutely breathtaking on each of them. Ken went above and beyond, securing an antique Rolls Royce to transport us to the reception after the ceremony. He even created personalized booklets for each member of the wedding party, meticulously outlining the schedule, directions, and other pertinent details. It was a thoughtful gesture, but sometimes I wondered who had the time for all this meticulous planning. Thankfully, Jill and Mom were immensely helpful during the bridesmaid luncheon held at our house. My cousins took charge of the preparations, and we delighted in a day filled with laughter, savoring chicken salad and petit fours while indulging in light and bubbly conversation.

Just days before the wedding, a card arrived in the mail, and the familiar handwriting on the envelope immediately caught my attention. Though there was no return address, I knew it was from Jax. For a moment, I hesitated, unsure of how I should proceed. Opening it meant potentially stirring up long-buried emotions. Placing the card on my bureau, I decided to wait and see what it contained. But curiosity soon got the better of me, and with my heart pounding in my chest, I carefully tore open the envelope postmarked Nepal and extracted the card. It was a simple card with a picturesque image of a meadow adorned with red poppies on the front. Inside, Jax had written a heartfelt message:

Dear Kate,

On location in Nepal with Time Magazine, it is so beautiful you would love it!

I think, sometimes the only sense you can make out of life is a sense of humor. All I've ever wanted is for you to be happy. Congratulations. I love you so much, Nugget!

Always,

Jax

A whirlwind of emotions washed over me, ranging from longing to sadness to anger. How dare he send this now? Jax wasn't even in Texas; he was off pursuing his career as a photojournalist around the globe. The last update I had received placed him in Asia, where he captured a powerful photograph of two young boys toiling as slaves, carrying stone blocks in the Himalayas. The image was featured in Time magazine, providing me with the only glimpse into his whereabouts. Jax was well on his way to a successful photography career, always on the move, capturing stories through his lens. I crumpled the note up and threw it away. A moment later I am retrieving it and flattening it out.

The rehearsal dinner, hosted by the Burnett family, was a lavish affair that almost outshone the wedding itself. It was a grand display with steak and lobster, silver domes, and an air of opulence that left my family thoroughly impressed. The event served as a momentary distraction, redirecting my focus toward Ken and our impending nuptials, which seemed to be approaching at lightning speed. Meanwhile, Ken reveled in the spotlight, relishing every moment of attention. He basked in it, as if savoring his taste of fame, and it brought a smile to my face. He was truly enjoying the whole experience.

The following day, the Burnett family treated my family to dinner, during which Ken planned to reveal our honeymoon destination. We hadn't discussed it, so I was in for a surprise. Just before we began eating, Ken presented me with a large box and instructed me to open it. I did, pulling out a bottle of water, a container of sand, and a windbreaker. Then he challenged me to guess our destination. After a few failed attempts, he handed me a brochure of Monte Carlo and a photograph of the stunning Hermitage Hotel, where we would be staying. His excitement was palpable as he chuckled with anticipation, announcing, "We're flying into Nice and taking a helicopter to Monte Carlo." The place I had always dreamed of visiting was becoming a reality. With a smile, I expressed my elation to Ken, who continued, "Our suite overlooks the water and provides a view of the castle and all the yachts docked at the port." I could almost imagine the beauty of the azure ocean and the picturesque surroundings, feeling a hint of the sea breeze tousling my hair. My dreams were indeed coming true.

As the topic of our honeymoon arose, Ken mentioned that his brother, Robert, was known as a "honeymoon baby" as he was born shortly after Forrest and Maureen returned from their own honeymoon. Forrest shared a humorous anecdote about people at their church asking him when he and Maureen got married because she seemed to be showing just three months after the wedding. It was then that I discovered the reason behind the label "honeymoon baby" for Robert.

Aunt Evie, who had indulged in a few glasses of red wine, was seated next to me. Suddenly, she nudged me with her elbow and whispered, "Bull. Maureen was already pregnant – she trapped him. We pulled their wedding together in three weeks. Honeymoon baby, my ass!" She then revealed that it was family secret number one and that I might as well get used to such revelations.

No wonder Aunt Evie had always been tough on Maureen. Had she trapped Forrest into marriage, or was it simply an unexpected surprise? Evie constantly criticized Maureen for not contributing to the family, emphasizing that she had never held a job in her life. Maureen had gone straight from her parents' house to Forrest's, and Evie never let her forget it.

What was I getting myself into? There was a vast difference between dating into this family and committing to it through marriage with Ken. Aunt Evie chuckled and jokingly informed me that they had a "no return" policy once Ken and I tied the knot.

Thankfully, the wedding proceeded flawlessly. The videographer captured every precious moment, showcasing the beauty of the stained glass in the church and the inviting warmth created by the dark mahogany benches bathed in candlelight. Ken couldn't hold back his tears during the ceremony, and I couldn't help but wish my father were there.

Walking down the aisle, guided by a path of delicate red rose petals, felt like a fairytale come true. The back of the program held a heartfelt letter I had written to my father, expressing my love for Ken and hoping for his blessings from Heaven. Many attendees commented on the touching inclusion of the letter.

The reception transformed into a grand celebration, with abundant food stations offering an array of delectable treats. We decided to cut the cake early, setting the stage for a night filled with joyous dancing. There was an electric excitement in the air, carrying the hopes for a lifelong marriage.

When the time came to bid farewell, the Rolls Royce pulled up outside the Country Club, and Ken and I embraced everyone, expressing our goodbyes. Suddenly, confetti filled the air. The groomsmen playfully showered Ken with an abundance of it, resulting in confetti finding its way into his hair, shirt, and even his pants. It was a hysterical moment! We were both covered in glitter and confetti, a cheerful reminder of the joyful celebration. The remnants of confetti even managed to find their way into our luggage!

After the reception, we checked into the Grove Park Inn in Asheville, where we would spend our first two nights as Mr. and Mrs. Kenneth Burnett. Exhausted from the whirlwind of our wedding, we ended up sleeping for most of the first day. The following morning, we made our way to the airport, eagerly embarking on our journey to Monte Carlo for our romantic honeymoon.

CHAPTER 7

inally, our journey was underway. The flight from Asheville to Atlanta was uneventful, but once we departed for London's Heathrow airport, we encountered some turbulent weather over the Atlantic. Ken, not typically nervous about flying, felt a bit queasy due to the turbulence and overall discomfort. Just before landing, he unexpectedly vomited into the seat pocket in front of him and then glanced at me nonchalantly, as if nothing had happened. Needless to say, I was relieved when we touched down so I could gather myself before continuing our journey to France.

From Heathrow, we boarded a direct flight to Nice. Upon arrival, we hopped into a helicopter that Ken had arranged, which whisked us away to Monte Carlo, landing on the rooftop of our hotel! Exhausted but filled with excitement, we made our way to our suite, where a thoughtful welcome basket from Forrest and Maureen awaited us on the bed.

Having been generously tipped by Ken in advance, the hotel staff treated us like royalty, catering to our every need. Moments after settling in, I called room service to request coffee, and it arrived promptly. It was at that moment that I realized how easily I could grow accustomed to this level of service, sparking my love affair with hotels and room service.

Ken had arranged for massages at the spa to help us relax after the journey. When we arrived at the front desk to check-in, we were informed that they had both male and female massage therapists available. Although we had requested two female therapists, Ken graciously insisted that I take the woman while he would be fine with the male therapist. After our massages, we changed into luxurious robes provided by the hotel and lounged on the couches, awaiting our next appointment in the treatment rooms.

Later that day, we decided to go for a drive in a rented Maserati. It was a beautiful day, and the scenery was breathtaking. I wanted to capture every moment, so I snapped pictures of the castle, the ocean, and the magnificent yachts in the harbor. In the evening, we enjoyed a delightful dinner at Louis IV and then headed to the casino. Outside, we marveled at the sight of some of the most expensive cars in the world, and we boldly parked our rented car among them. Ken thoroughly enjoyed admiring the cars, but security was tight due to the presence of high rollers inside the casino. It was the first time I had ever felt a sense of relative financial modesty.

Upon returning to the hotel that night, Ken left me in the room while he dropped off the film from our camera to be developed overnight. He then ventured out for some shopping. I decided to relax and watch a movie, ordering room service for dinner. The following morning, after a delightful breakfast overlooking the ocean and witnessing the arrival of cruise ships, Ken went to retrieve our developed pictures. When he returned, he was furious because none of the photos had turned out. They were all overexposed due to damage sustained by the camera during the trip. I was taken aback by Ken's anger, as I had never seen him so upset. He surprised me further by calling his mother to vent his frustrations and express his dissatisfaction.

That day, we revisited all the original photo spots and captured the pictures again with a brand-new camera. I couldn't quite comprehend the significance Ken placed on it, but I wanted to avoid another outburst during our honeymoon. It felt peculiar when he insisted I change outfits, just so the photos would appear to be taken on different days.

During the remaining days of our trip, we cherished leisurely breakfasts on the balcony, savoring the picturesque view of the harbor and the shimmering Mediterranean Sea. Ken meticulously planned our activities while I basked in the beauty of the French Riviera. One memorable day, he surprised me by chartering a yacht, and we sailed along the breathtaking coastline, catching glimpses of Italy in the distance.

But as the saying goes, all good things must come to an end. We bid farewell to Monte Carlo and embarked on our journey back home. Arriving in Asheville, Ken and I headed straight to our house. I had already moved in prior to the wedding, aiming to settle in beforehand. Ken's mother had arranged for his belongings to be moved while we were away, ensuring a functioning home upon our return. As a gesture of thoughtfulness, she had even stocked the non-perishable items on the kitchen counter, allowing us to see what she had bought.

The moment we stepped through the door, Maureen wasted no time pointing out that I needed to clean out my closets. It struck me as odd, as she could only make such a remark if she had thoroughly inspected each and every one of them. Opting to keep my thoughts to myself, I quietly retreated to the back of the house, seeking solitude. Meanwhile, Maureen and Ken engaged in conversation while I unpacked, eager to prepare for my upcoming job and excited to embrace my new role as Ken's wife.

That evening, we had dinner with Ken's family. As we sat at the table, Aunt Evie launched into her familiar tale of her late husband's dedication to the business he loved. Glancing at Maureen, I could see her disinterest, likely thinking, "Here we go again." Forrest held his sister in high regard due to her business acumen, often allowing her to retell the story.

Her sarcastic wit was sharp, and nobody wanted to become the target of her biting remarks.

I found myself wondering how Evie acquired the nickname "Tiger Shark" within the timber industry. Lost in thought, I began to daydream about her embodying the essence of that formidable predator. My college studies in marine ecosystems had taught me about the tiger shark's fierce nature, its position as a top predator in the water, and the inherent danger it posed to humans. I also recalled the disturbing fact that tiger shark embryos would sometimes cannibalize their littermates, with the largest embryo consuming all but one of its siblings. In the depths of my mind, I privately referred to Evie as "Aunt Evil," thinking to myself, "Wow, that's 'Aunt Evil' indeed!"

Abruptly, I became aware of the silence at the table, accompanied by everyone's gaze fixed upon me. Evie, with her penetrating blue eyes and venomous tongue, rasped, "I see you've set aside this special time to humiliate yourself in public." She continued to prod, "Well, speak up, Kate, are you in a coma?"

Completely embarrassed, my cheeks burned hotter, and I couldn't help but wonder if everyone else was aware of my mortification. With a dry mouth, I managed to mumble, "I apologize, Aunt Evie."

In an effort to integrate me into the Burnett family business, Forrest took me under his wing to teach me the ropes. He appeared to be genuinely impressed with how quickly I grasped the intricacies of the timber industry. One day, he gathered the team in the boardroom and urged us to envision the exact position we wanted the company to achieve. After the meeting, Forrest took me aside and elaborated on the role he wanted me to assume.

He explained that one of his primary responsibilities was to find the right forestry consultant to select the best trees for harvesting. Additionally, he wanted me to learn the art of finding buyers for the timber and obtaining competitive bids to secure the best possible price. Ken had initially been tasked with this job, but his affable nature lacked the necessary follow-through to close deals.

On the other hand, I found myself excelling in sales effortlessly. Asking for the order came naturally to me, and I had no reservations about guiding potential buyers through the sales process, often with minimal intervention from Forrest. I also found success in attending timber auctions, where I would navigate the bidding process and ultimately select the winning bid. Once terms were agreed upon, I would secure the buyer's signature on the contract.

Forrest admired my ability to sell in a way that made buyers feel as if they hadn't been "sold" but rather had their problems solved. Employing consultative sales techniques, I approached buyers as if they had a problem in need of a solution—and I provided that solution. This approach allowed me to surpass sales quotas with ease. Forrest took pride in my innate sales skills and boasted about me to the entire family, proudly claiming to have a new protégé. Our bond grew stronger as a result.

However, Maureen and Aunt Evie were far from pleased with my newfound success, despite the substantial profits I brought to the company. They resented the attention Forrest showered upon me and were unhappy with the protection that came with it. With me becoming the new shining star in Forrest's eyes, they felt threatened. Aunt Evie, who had always prided herself on getting things done in the company, didn't want any competition or new talent that could potentially dethrone her. She possessed extensive knowledge of the rules governing the timber industry, including the hundred rules developed to account for log taper, saw kerf, and the process of removing wood for slabs. It was her responsibility to maintain an accurate inventory of the trees.

Meanwhile, Maureen's jealousy intensified as she saw the attention I received from Forrest. Having never held a job herself and being a full-time stay-at-home mom, she couldn't help but feel envious. Unbeknownst to me, an alliance formed between Aunt Evie and Maureen against me simply because I excelled at my work. This alliance set in motion a series of troubling incidents during family gatherings. It felt like the frog in the kettle story, where the frog is placed in cool water and gradually heated until it's boiling, realizing the danger too late. Well, I was that frog, blissfully unaware of the simmering tensions around me.

The Burnetts had a tradition of celebrating birthdays once a month, gathering for dinner and cake to honor family members with birthdays. On a particular Sunday afternoon, the family had assembled to celebrate birthdays, so I reached out to Maureen and asked if there was anything I could bring. She replied with a "No" since they were planning to have a pizza night.

When Ken and I entered the house, we were greeted by Evie and Maureen, who I jokingly referred to as the "hot-flash tactical team." Immediately, Maureen asked me to join her in the kitchen to help with ordering the pizzas—one large with all the toppings, including anchovies, and one large cheese pizza. The idea of anchovies didn't sit well with me, so I double-checked the order with Maureen, specifically asking about the anchovies. She confirmed the order, and I proceeded to call the local pizza place to place the order.

Once the pizza arrived, Maureen paid the delivery driver and brought the boxes into the kitchen, calling everyone to gather for dinner. She then opened the boxes, picked up a slice, and exclaimed, "Oh no, this isn't right! It has anchovies on it." She announced to everyone in the kitchen that I must have made a mistake in the order and instructed them to put anchovies on the pizza. The room filled with groans, and Forrest chimed in, saying, "It smells like fish. I'm not eating that!" Maureen then "saved the day" by retrieving a honey-baked ham and fresh rolls from the fridge, declaring, "Take that pizza out to the trash and throw it away. It's stinking up the kitchen."

Immediately, I questioned her, stating, "You told me to put anchovies on it. I even asked you about it." Her response was dismissive, "Then you obviously didn't listen very well, Dear." In that instant, I realized that she had deliberately done this to provoke me. Something broke Maureen years ago, probably putting up with Forrest all these years. I thought to myself, "So this is how it's going to be." I could only imagine what Aunt Evie thought, likely considering me an amateur in handling their family dynamics.

Later that night, Ken and I had a lengthy conversation. As I tried to explain my side of the story, he listened but remained silent. He didn't seem surprised or particularly concerned, treating it as no big deal. I quickly learned that Ken shared everything with his mother, so she had won once again by obtaining a detailed account of how the incident affected me. I had really messed up this time. Maureen had made sure we were alone when she instructed me to order the pizza. The old lady was more cunning than I had given her credit for. My mind just didn't work in that manipulative way. I never went out of my way to plan revenge or humiliate others. I was fairly certain that Evie had subjected Maureen to similar hazing in the past, and now I was tied to the whipping post. It seemed to be my turn to endure this stupidity.

A change of scenery was necessary, so Jill and I decided to treat ourselves to a mani-pedi and not let the Burnett family ruin our weekend. We headed to the spa at the Grove Park Inn for the day, enjoying side-by-side pedicures while engaging in conversation. Since Jill was my guest, Ken had already paid for her visit before we arrived.

Jill and Travis were eagerly anticipating the arrival of their twins, a boy and a girl, which meant Jill's belly was growing bigger every day. It brought joy to see the nursery taking shape with two of everything. They had decided on the names Sam and Shelby for their son and daughter. It was comforting to know that Jill lived nearby, and that we could spend time together. Being a nurse, she had the flexibility to work as needed or desired, always finding the right nursing job to fit her needs.

Things continued to go well for me at work, and I thoroughly enjoyed the art of selling. Closing a deal gave me an incredible high, and I consistently outperformed Ken. In fact, I ended up assisting him with the advertising side of the business by hiring a marketing assistant who effectively did Ken's job. However, we kept this arrangement discreet and didn't let anyone else know.

Ken had a distinct preference for custom-made clothing from the Tom Jones Company. The sales representative would visit our office regularly, helping coordinate and maintain Ken's wardrobe. The rep would bring in fabrics and make recommendations for Ken's outfits. We shared an office space with two desks, so when the sales rep arrived, Ken would close the door to allow him to take measurements. The whole process seemed peculiar to me as I was content with buying off-the-rack clothing from a store. But for Ken, nothing but the best would do. He was always boasting about his purchases or orders. Changing cars frequently, it was hard to keep track of what he was driving. He had a genuine passion for automobiles and his favorite magazine was Car and Driver.

The Country Club mirrored the exclusivity and elitism that defined its membership. Admission was by private invitation only, and candidates had to undergo a voting process before being allowed to join. The Biltmore Forest Country Club held the prestigious title of a Platinum Club of America, an honor bestowed upon only the top three percent of private clubs. The Burnetts had connections with the membership director, which made them highly involved in the membership elections. It also provided Aunt Evie an avenue to stay up-to-date with the gossip and affairs of the elite. She mingled with the upper crust of society and was acquainted with everyone, while everyone knew her.

Ken and I resided in a new neighborhood close to the club, surrounded by ongoing construction. The community offered a chance to meet new couples through pool parties and encounters during dog walks. It was a planned community designed to foster a social environment. Each new homeowner had to be at or near the same economic level to gain entry into the neighborhood. All the families were new and eager to connect with one another. The neighborhood had a downtown area with restaurants and shops lining a brick road with sidewalks, making it an ideal place to raise children.

Impressing others was paramount to Ken, so he consistently made sure to drop his father's name when meeting new people. It started to bother me, so I once asked him why he did it. He reacted angrily, telling me not to tell him what to do. I was taken aback by his response and began to question his maturity level.

Something was amiss. It felt like there was a force field or an invisible wall between us, creating a sense of distance and Ken becoming increasingly critical of me. I couldn't pinpoint the exact cause of this change, and it left me feeling confused and disconnected from him.

CHAPTER 8

During the first year of our marriage, Ken seemed focused on checking off items from his to-do list, which included building our first house, joining the Biltmore Forest Country Club, leasing a Mercedes, and, according to him, producing an heir. We felt pressured by Ken's parents and Aunt Evie to have a baby. Aunt Evie even called me one day, prying into our personal lives and asking when we were planning to start a family, insinuating that we shouldn't be using birth control. Although it was none of her business, I told her that we had been trying to have a baby for six months without success.

As time passed and we struggled to conceive, Ken's impatience grew. He insisted that I go to the lab for a blood test every month just to check. After a few months, we decided to seek help from a fertility clinic, and our sex life became non-existent, a clinical process involving artificial insemination where Ken submitted a vial of sperm for the doctor to use. It was more of a science experiment than an intimate connection. The whole ordeal consumed my thoughts, and I started doubting my ability to get pregnant.

The fertility specialist informed us that I had an extremely small uterus and Ken had fertility issues, with "slow swimmers." He suggested that getting me pregnant through artificial insemination would be relatively possible, but carrying a baby to term might not be advisable. My uterus was just too small. My ordeal with severe endometriosis and scarring made the process much harder.

We moved on, deciding to adopt a baby using an agency called Life For kids. It only took five months for a baby to be matched to us. The birth mother was pregnant and wanted to place her baby girl up for adoption. The agency adoption counselor called to tell me and I wanted to surprise Ken with the news we had been matched. The Burnett's thought this may be a great plan because lots of couples get pregnant right after adopting a baby since it takes the pressure off.

After being told a baby was on the way and we would be able to adopt her once she was born, I started planning the surprise and let Ken know we got the call.

I went to a baby boutique downtown and bought pink and blue blocks and a baby swing. I spelled out "BABY" and hung the swing in a tree in our backyard. When Ken saw it, he started crying and immediately called his mother. The news quickly spread through the family, even before Ken had a chance to fully process it himself. It was impossible to keep a secret in that family. Robert told Forest before we could. At least I had the chance to tell my mom and Jill first. Maureen was excited and eager to go shopping for a crib. Ken had his heart set on a round dark wood crib, so that's what she bought. It was a joyful time, with a baby shower and preparations for the nursery while we waited for the birth of the baby.

Preparing for a little girl was an exciting experience. My friends Maggie and Belinda were also pregnant at the same time, so we were all going through the journey of having kids about the same time.

Marriage felt different from our courtship days. The engagement, wedding, and honeymoon were filled with excitement and energy, but I wondered how we could maintain that spark. Ken's focus shifted from our relationship to material acquisitions and status. The initial infatuation had faded, and the early dating passion seemed to have disappeared. I craved closeness and intimacy, but that deeper level of connection that grows over time was elusive. I initially attributed it to the strain of our fertility struggles, which had taken a toll on our sex life. But now that we were adopting a little girl, Ken still avoided any physical contact, not even a hug. Why wouldn't he touch me? It seemed as if he didn't want anything to do with me physically since I could not get pregnant.

Tonya McBean

We had chosen the name Emma for our baby, and I was ready to embrace motherhood, but Ken's behavior grew more distant. He was set on having a son and was not as excited about a daughter it seemed because he wanted a son to carry on the family name.

I simply thought this was a bumpy patch. It made me wonder if I needed new clothes or to get fitter? Mom had bought me a few things, but there was not enough hair and lipstick to cover the distance between Ken and I. Ken always had a crowd around him and was very concerned about what others thought. Therefore, he was naturally concerned about the clothes that I wore and how I looked. He constantly told me what to wear.

The country club was a very important part of our social life. It was where we met friends for dinner, worked out, and was a place where Ken could conduct business. We played pickleball and golf. In fact, we spent about as much time there as we did at home. Ken was very friendly and he had to know everyone. He was a name- dropper and always knew the latest gossip. Because he was so affable, people talked to him and told him everything. That is how he knew the scoop on everyone at the club, everyone in the church, and even the people in our neighborhood. The Biltmore Country Club was founded in 1922 and was invitation only. Nothing like the relaxed country club Jill and I grew up in.

Ken treated me like a queen when we were around people outside of the family. He was so attentive that other women would become envious and want their husbands to be like him.

However, his behavior would quickly change as soon as the car doors closed for the dreaded drive home. He would begin to nit- pick and criticize everything I had said and done. We were still new in our marriage and I didn't want to fight with him, so I kept quiet. Besides, I knew that I could never win an argument with his narcissistic tendencies.

One night I wasn't feeling well and Ken really got under my skin. I unloaded on him: "In case you haven't noticed the only person who doesn't think I am delightful and funny is you. Everyone likes me and tolerates you. You are always showing off and dropping your dad's name into any conversation you can. Be your own man!" Ken did not speak to me after this, giving me the silent treatment.

Ken was such a pampered pup that no one had ever served it back to him like I did that night. I was furious and just had to say what was on my mind. We drove in silence to the house and then I immediately got out and went to the master suite to take a long, hot bath. The bubbles almost spilled over the tub and the candles I lit put a beautiful glow all over the bathroom. I needed to feel pampered that night because there was something wrong. That evening at the club I ran into JoAnne Taylor. The first thing she asked was if I had heard the news that Jax was married. I felt like she punched me in the face. Flushed with embarrassment and a host of other emotions, I hurried to the ladies' room and quickly found a stall, and shut the door. Ken couldn't see me like this, especially because it involved Jax! I was crushed.

In the quiet solitude of my bubble bath, I allowed myself to process my emotions. I knew it was irrational to expect Jax to remain unmarried. I wondered what his new wife was like and how Jax was faring in Texas. Eventually, I began to relax in the warm water and pondered whether his new wife truly understood what an incredible person Jax was. Deep down, I acknowledged that Ken would never compare to Jax, but I had foolishly believed that anything man could fill the void in my heart that Jax had left behind. That place in my heart was still tender. I learned that you never truly forget your first love. But the connections I had with Jax were special.

Both Jax and I were to blame. We loved each other too much to tear each other away from our respective families. I had always believed that if I left my family to be with Jax, he would lose respect for me. He had an unwavering loyalty toward his own family. Now, we were both married to other people, and I was adopting a baby with Ken. I had a different life now, and I found happiness in being with Jill and my mom. North Carolina was the life I had chosen, so it was time to embrace it fully and let Jax go.

The following morning, Ken and I sat in silence while sipping our coffee before getting ready for church. We attended a large church, and Sunday mornings were always a bustling social event. It was expected of both of our families to be present. Despite feeling peculiar, I mustered the energy to dress for church. On the way there, what Jill and I jokingly referred to as the "pep rally," I immediately informed Ken, that I was bleeding and had sharp pain in my stomach. Ken seemed more concerned about the leather seats in the Mercedes than my well-being. He was still not speaking to me. In the midst of my agitation, I snapped at him, yelling, "I'm really bleeding!"

Upon reaching the emergency room, Ken left the car running, hastily exited, and rushed inside in his usual self-centered manner. The attendants swiftly came to my aid upon noticing the presence of blood on my dress. I regained consciousness to find Ken sitting in a chair beside my hospital bed.

It was the second time in my life that this had happened, but unlike the first, there were no flowers, and an unsettling feeling hung in the air. When I inquired what went wrong I noticed Jill and Mom positioned at the foot of the bed. Ken spoke up, his voice trembling and tears streaming down his face, "You had urgent surgery." Then he delivered the devastating news, "We can't ever have any children." He explained that the obstetrician had to perform a hysterectomy due to a torn uterus and significant blood loss. The surgery saved my life. I knew that the doctors said I should not have children but just realized that Ken wanted to try to have kids even if I was endangered in the pregnancy.

As I lay there, gazing at Ken with my mother holding my hand, a mix of emotions washed over me. Numbness, anger, and a sense of being cheated intertwined within me. It was time to let this go. The endometriosis had been stage four which caused the bleeding and I had all four types and the surgery was necessary.

I healed from the hysterectomy and had time to recover before we got Emma.

We really got excited about Emma after her birth mother signed the papers. It was starting to seem real. However, above all, I was filled with joy that Emma was safe and thriving in foster care. After a prolonged silence, I voiced the thought that dominated my mind: "God has a plan."

Holding Emma for the first time, my world changed. She was five days old and a tiny little peanut. Life was no longer about me, it was about her.

Emma's birth mother was in college in Orlando, Florida. She studied art. She was Jewish, 18, and had long light brown hair and accidently got pregnant and decided not to tell anyone but her parents. She placed the baby up for adoption without letting other people know, including the birth father whom she slept with during Christmas/Hanukkah break in New York. She went back to college in Florida and discovered she was pregnant.

She did not go home during her pregnancy to keep it under wraps so she stayed at college and delivered the baby at Winter Park hospital in perfect health. She. It was a closed adoption so we did not learn her name or meet the birth mother. The birth mother refused to give the birth fathers name or any information about the birth father. I am grateful she didn't choose abortion because she gave me Emma.

Emma was a delightful baby, full of life and charm. Ken and I couldn't have orchestrated anything as special as her. To top it off, she displayed remarkable intelligence, speaking in complete sentences by the age of 18 months. I poured my heart and soul into being the best mother I could be for our precious daughter, and I discovered my natural aptitude for it. Emma and I bonded instantly. I was looking at the paperwork from the agency and included within the papers was a certificate with Emma's footprints on it from the hospital. I flipped it over and on the back was the name J. Pinilis. I realized this was the birth mothers name. It was written on the back probably by a nurse and since the baby had no name they needed to know who the footprints belonged to. It must have been included by mistake. I put the paper in Emma's baby book and wondered if the birth mother thought about the beautiful baby she gave up.

With her dark hair adorned with ringlets and her flawless, creamy complexion, Emma resembled a little doll. I adored styling her hair, often gathering it into a small ponytail and securing it with a large bow on top of her head. Her beautiful blue eyes framed her tiny face. I hired a painter to apply Venetian Plaster in the dining room, as it was all the rage at the time. In his charming English accent, the painter remarked, "You are the spitting image of your mother."

Emma looked at me with curiosity and asked, "What does that mean, Mommy?" I replied, "It means our faces look alike." She then observed, "Except mine is smooth." The painter and I exchanged smiles, captivated by Emma's innocence. It was a God wink that Emma looked so much like me even though she was adopted. Most of the time I forget and people assumed she was mine.

Ken insisted on grand birthday parties for Emma, and Christmas celebrations were always extravagant. He even hired a Santa Claus to visit our home each year, bringing cheer to Emma and capturing a photo with her.

Annually, Ken would have me take Emma to a professional studio to have her pictures taken in a garden setting. We carefully selected the perfect shot, which the photographer would stretch onto canvas and transform into a beautiful print. Though it was an expensive and ostentatious display, we always proudly exhibited a current portrait of Emma above the fireplace. Ken adored it.

For our Christmas cards, we consistently featured a picture of Emma created by the same studio. One year, the studio owner reached out to Ken, asking if they could hang a canvas photo portrait of Emma in their studio as an advertisement. Ken was thrilled at the idea and eagerly accepted. He enthusiastically shared the news with everyone, taking pride in Emma's selection.

Undoubtedly, Ken's passion for spreading the word about the photographer resulted in increased bookings for them. His talent for promotion was unmatched. Every time we walked downtown, we couldn't help but pass by the studio, with Emma's portrait prominently displayed in their shop window.

As Emma turned three, Ken's focus shifted to wanting another child, specifically a son to carry on the family name. His father Forrest was almost pushing us for another adoption and a son. Ken researched adoption agencies and specified that we wanted a healthy "Gerber" baby with no mental or physical issues, even if it required additional expenses and screening.

Throughout our marriage, Ken rarely considered my desires or opinions. It was always about what he wanted, and I often went along with it. However, I was content with Emma and didn't feel the need for anything else. She fulfilled my need for love, and I believed that my heart had room to love another child. Love does not divide, it multiples. I always believed you could never have too many people love you. Seeing our friends having their second babies made it feel like a natural stage of life to consider expanding our family.

My mother called from Charleston and suggested that adopting a boy would be okay and would prevent a girl baby from being "Emma's ugly little sister." Emma was beautiful so I chuckled. Since Emma was such an easy child, I thought motherhood was a breeze. I considered myself a good mother and followed all the advice offered in baby books. Emma was almost effortless.

Then one day, Forrest said he received information about a one- year-old blond-haired, blue-eyed boy who was available for adoption. Ken was hell bent on having a son so Forrest must have known this would be an easy sell. If the birth mother signed the papers, he could be ours in three weeks. We decided to name him Logan Parker Burnett, keeping his first name as it was to avoid confusion. Forrest stayed in close contact with the baby's mother and family working out the monetary details and we hoped for a positive outcome. We believed that if it was meant to be, it would work out.

Unbeknownst to me at the time, Ken's parents had seen Logan while he was still in foster care with his mom, before we even had the opportunity to meet him. Ken knew about this, but he kept it from me. Forrest seemed overly involved with the boy's adoption. However, it didn't bother me much at the time. I was fully engrossed in taking care of Emma and spending time with my friends and their children. The presence of Ken and his control in my life no longer grated on my nerves. I was genuinely happy and content with the choices I had made. Emma had filled a void that Ken seemed incapable or unwilling to fill. I accepted this and acknowledged that he was unable to provide me with the support and attention I needed. Nonetheless, he was trying to be a good father to Emma. At least he wasn't mean to her like he was with me.

Emma and my family brought me immense joy and fulfillment. I couldn't ask for more. Now, we were eagerly preparing for Logan to join our family. Emma was thrilled about having a baby brother and asked what he would be like. Ken barely even spoke to me. When he wasn't traveling, he would go into his office and shut the door. I was told his office was off-limits so he could focus.

CHAPTER 9

After adopting Logan, my life took on a new level of busyness. With both Emma and Logan, it felt like I was always rushing from one place to another. Ken was frequently absent, so I relied heavily on my family and friends for support. Despite the constant busyness, I found immense joy in being a mother to both Logan and Emma, even though it left me with little time for myself. But Forrest always made time for Logan almost in a strange way.

When Logan reached the age of two, the infamous "terrible twos" hit with full force. Tantrums and defiant behavior seemed to come in waves. However, despite the challenging moments, Logan still had his endearing side. He loved to snuggle and insisted on being carried.

Logan had an attachment to his blanket, which he affectionately called his "blank-blank." He carried it everywhere and became upset if he didn't have it. One Sunday at church, the nursery worker informed us that Logan couldn't bring his blanket anymore because he was using it to capture and tackle other children. This incident embarrassed Maureen, so she insisted we wean Logan off the blanket. Logan was also a thumb-sucker, and he would hold his blanket in the other hand as a source of comfort. We gradually cut the blanket into smaller pieces, starting with four big squares and continuing until it was in small strips. This solution allowed Logan to continue having his comfort item while eliminating the problem of the large blanket.

One day, while talking to Jill on the phone, I shared some of Logan's mischievous adventures. He had flushed a ball down the toilet, sprayed Lysol foam bathroom cleaner into his mouth, knocked over the hamster cage, thrown his shirt in the pool, stuck his finger in poop during a diaper change, put a tic-tac up his nose, painted his hands with red fingernail polish, and stained his teeth and lips black by biting an ink pen refill. It seemed that his behavior was becoming more extreme. Jill, always patient, simply listened. I couldn't express how much I needed that understanding from her.

During Christmas, Jill and Travis had a family photo taken with their 6-year-old twins, Sam and Shelby. Sam had a black eye because Logan had punched him. On the first day of Mom's Day Out, I had dressed Logan in a Polo shirt and shorts, and when I briefly left to brush Emma's hair, I returned to find him holding a black magic marker. He had used it to draw all over his face and even inside his ear.

Emma and I burst into laughter. It was clear that I couldn't let Logan out of my sight for even a minute.

Logan's behavior continued to escalate, and I grew weary of people attributing it to the "terrible twos." In comparison to Logan, Emma was well-behaved and easy to parent. Logan was wild and displayed a natural talent for sports. We bought a small basketball goal for him in an attempt to channel his energy. Looking back, I realize that keeping him active was essential to help him expend some of his excess energy. I was exhausted from the lack of sleep at night and constantly cleaning up after his messes. He would engage in random acts like climbing on the sink and squirting lotion everywhere, or squeezing his juice box to spray juice all over the kitchen. I once went to use the restroom and when I returned, I found him outside standing on an overturned garbage can, using scissors to cut the bushes. Although the backyard was fenced and he was safe, I had to watch him every second.

Emma was completely different from Logan. She was obedient, and at the same age, I could leave her unattended to watch television for fifteen minutes or longer. I understood that boys and girls could have different temperaments, but I began to wonder if there was something else going on, like ADHD.

Over time, Logan's behavior became increasingly uncontrollable, and he had daily tantrums. He was never a good sleeper and started to wander at night. One night, a neighbor returned home at two in the morning and discovered Logan outside in the driveway, riding his tricycle with his new flashlight. When Jill asked me about Ken's reaction, I told her that he was furious, but not at Logan—at me! Jill couldn't understand why Ken blamed me and said that he should have been just as responsible since he was at home sleeping, just like me. I explained that neither of us heard Logan leave the house, and the garage door had been left open.

Out of anger and concern, Ken decided to turn the doorknob around on Logan's door and lock him in his room at night. He also installed high locks on the doors and we started using the alarm system during the night. Jill was shocked to hear about all of this and wondered why I hadn't shared it with her earlier. I explained that Ken didn't want anyone to know. He wouldn't even discuss Logan's behavior or address it with him because he believed I was to blame for not being a good mother. This led to more arguments between us, as I firmly believed I was doing everything in my power to address Logan's behavior. The pressure to be perfect every single day was hard. Ken was hard, Logan was hard. Jill became my confidant, someone I could trust and talk to about anything. Having her on my side provided comfort and a voice of reason.

At times, Logan would wake up at two in the morning screaming and calling out. I would rush into his room to prevent him from waking Emma, and then spend hours trying to get him settled back to sleep. I was beyond exhausted. Our pediatrician, who also happened to be our neighbor, would dismiss my concerns, laughing and saying that Logan was just a typical two-year-old boy. It was impossible to explain everything in a brief, routine doctor visit that lasted only a few minutes.

The challenges with Logan's behavior extended beyond the home and into the car. Putting him in his car seat would result in screaming and him biting my hands. Since Emma was in school, I shared a carpool with three other moms. One day, Logan spit on one of the little girls as she was getting into the back of the SUV. I was mortified. Within a week, two of the mothers dropped out of the carpool due to Logan's behavior. On the last day with a full car, Logan took off his tennis shoe and threw it at me, hitting me in the back of my head. All the kids laughed, so he threw the other shoe. The following day, I made sure to keep the windows locked, and I stopped putting his shoes on until we arrived at our destination. Ken offered no help with the kids, leaving all the responsibility to me.

I couldn't help but reflect on the day we adopted Logan and how excited we were to welcome him into our family. Forest and Maureen brought him over to meet us and said everything was taken care of and it was all done. Ken was thrilled to have a son who would carry on the family name to please his father, and Emma was excited to have a baby brother.

Forest was over the moon happy but Maureen did not seem to be. She said to me, " Watch out, Logan is more of a Burnett than you are. It was a weird statement. I mean he is the heir and all.

Logan's birth mother Emily Searcy was living with her because she had run away from her parents' household, and her grandparents eventually reached a point where they could no longer deal with Emily and made her get a job. The Burnett's had hired Emily as one of their housekeepers. Emily had an unintended pregnancy, no means to really support a child, or desire to be a mother and decided to give the toddler up for adoption, Forrest explained. That's when Forest came up with the idea to get him for us.

Forrest said he expressed to Emily how much of a gift it was to adopt her boy, and she simply thanked him with her eyes averted to the floor. Then I mentioned how God had turned a difficult situation in her life into a positive one for our family. Ken, trying to hold back his emotions, didn't say much either. He seemed like he was really somewhere else.

Logan's mother handed him over to Forst, and then we were told she left town. He appeared small for his age. His blond white hair was fuzzy and slightly static, but there was no sadness in his blue eyes. He seemed comfortable with us, and, true to form, his blanket was close by while he sucked his thumb.

When Forest handed Logan to me, he settled in and let me hold him. Logan hadn't started speaking much yet, but he was an adorable child. Ken was crying, and the Burnett's, who covered the adoption costs with Emily, were thrilled that our family was now complete. Logan was a loving child, and we were amazed at how quickly he took to all of us, particularly Emma. He loved chasing her around, bringing joy to our lives.

Logan's room was decorated with a sports theme, filled with sports equipment like a golf club, tennis racket, and boat oar hanging on the walls. The curtains featured metal grommets and a print of basketballs, footballs, and soccer balls, with blue denim trim to match the bedding. Toys were scattered everywhere, creating a little boy's dream space.

In the beginning, Logan referred to everyone as "Dada," regardless of who they were. It was adorable. He would often wake up during the night, and I would go in with a juice cup to rock him back to sleep. We anticipated that the transition of changing families would be challenging for him, so we didn't worry too much when he woke up crying every night.

The first few months were filled with love and family hugs, almost like a fantasy. Emma was fascinated with her new brother and was incredibly helpful. She enjoyed playing with him and watching Disney movies together. One night, Logan kept calling out, "Mommy! Mommy! Mommy!" I went in three times to check on him, give him goodnight kisses, and tell him to stop yelling "Mommy." He continued doing it for twenty minutes while I waited for him to tire himself out. Finally, I lost my patience and said, "Do not say Mommy again!" before walking out of his room and shutting the door. Suddenly, Logan exclaimed, "Kate! Kate! Kate!" and I couldn't help but burst out laughing.

Logan was a smart and lovable little boy, and we adored him so much. Nothing compares to the joy on your little boy's face when he says, "Mommy" and wraps his tiny arms around your neck. Logan had a loving and gentle side that could melt your heart. He was an affectionate child who had the ability to be kind and giving, that is, until something triggered his anger.

Emma was very kind to Logan, so we tried to help him understand the importance of being kind to her as well. However, dealing with Logan's difficult behavior consumed most of my time, leaving very little for Emma. Ken took Emma to social events, church activities, and school functions while I stayed home with Logan. Taking Logan anywhere was a challenge since he was prone to hitting and spitting at others. I had to be vigilant and watch him closely because when he became angry, he would try to bite me.

During this time, our marriage began to lose its spark. The most challenging part was that Ken seemed indifferent toward me, which was incredibly hard to bear. He was difficult to please and expected me to take care of and control Logan.

On one weekend, we went as a family to a pool party just three houses down. Logan had a hotdog and a hamburger and wanted to walk around with his plate, but I said, "No."

Without hesitation, he grabbed the plate and threw it into the pool, watching as buns floated alongside his chips. Anger surged through me, and I grabbed him and angrily marched back home. Meanwhile, Ken and Emma stayed at the party, leaving me to handle Logan's tantrum all by myself.

By the time I carried Logan home, sweat was dripping down my forehead. Desperate for a moment of respite, I decided to quickly jump in the shower, bringing him into the living room to watch TV. Just as I was lathering up, I caught a glimpse of Logan sneaking into the bathroom. A surge of anxiety rushed through me as I noticed the mischievous glint in his eyes. Without a moment's hesitation, he darted towards my closet, conveniently located next to the shower, and began hurling my high heels over the shower door. Within seconds, multiple pairs of shoes were flying in, while my pleas for him to stop turned into desperate screams. Overwhelmed by the situation, tears streamed down my face. With the water off, shampoo in my hair, and stinging soap in my eyes, I found myself sobbing uncontrollably. And amidst my tears, Logan's laughter only grew louder and more unrestrained.

Where was all of this leading? What was happening to my once beautiful little family? These questions gnawed at me, filling me with a deep sense of uncertainty and concern.

CHAPTER 10

Logan's troubling behavior seemed to escalate with each passing day, leaving me constantly on edge. It was challenging to gauge his emotional state or predict when he would reach a tipping point and become violent. Unlike Emma, whose emotions I could read in her eyes, Logan's sudden shifts in behavior left me feeling powerless and unsure.

After an exhausting day, Logan and I had both drifted off to sleep in the rocking chair. My mind, however, refused to rest. The realization that something was genuinely wrong with Logan weighed heavily on me. I knew that we needed to take action, but I felt overwhelmed and uncertain about what steps to take. In a moment of guilt, I gently lifted him and placed him in bed, silently praying that he would remain asleep.

Driven by my desperation for answers, I turned to the kitchen computer and began researching ADHD in young children. As I read about the symptoms, it became increasingly clear that seeking professional help was necessary. Despite knowing that Ken would likely resist the idea of taking Logan to a child psychiatrist, I was determined to pursue it. After all, Ken was rarely around and didn't have to face the daily challenges of dealing with Logan's difficult behavior. Whenever I tried discussing Logan's kicking and biting, Ken would simply blame me, insisting that I needed to be stricter. But I knew from experience that harsh discipline only made Logan angrier and harder to calm down, so I refused to resort to spanking. Besides, I had never needed to spank Emma; a firm voice had always been enough to correct her behavior.

One Sunday morning, a nursery worker at church approached Ken, urging him not to bring Logan back to the class. She explained that Logan's behavior was causing harm to the other children, with incidents of biting and hitting. The parents had even lodged complaints, and one little girl had been bitten on the cheek. The nursery worker emphasized that they needed a dedicated staff member to keep a close eye on Logan, making it challenging to properly attend to the other children. As an alternative, the children's ministry director offered a separate room for Logan, but one of us would need to stay with him during church activities.

During the church's Easter egg hunt, Logan went on a rampage, stomping on the eggs while the other children gathered them in their baskets. When I questioned his actions, he hissed, "I need to hit somebody." As we were leaving, Logan blocked a woman from opening the large glass door. When she pushed on the handle, causing the door to open and Logan to fall, he quickly retaliated by running over and spitting on her dress. Ken instructed him to apologize, but Logan pinched Ken and spit on his pants instead. Filled with rage, Ken swiftly carried Logan to the car, secured him in the car seat, and spat in his face, demanding, "So, how do you like that?" Emma began crying, and despite Ken's attempts to console her, she remained deeply upset.

The incidents at church and the escalating challenges with Logan's behavior only intensified the strain on our family. It was clear that our once harmonious dynamic was now fractured and in desperate need of resolution.

On the way home, Ken's anger towards me continued to escalate as he berated me about Logan and the events that had transpired. I desperately tried to explain to him that with Logan, I had no frame of reference for what was considered normal. Despite being a small child, I had to be on constant high alert, watching his every move as if he were a toddler. It felt like there was never a moment of respite.

Ken's infuriation grew so intense that it spiraled into a three-day argument where I had no chance of winning. Engaging in a fight with Ken felt futile, like fighting a losing battle. There was no way to find a resolution or bring any semblance of harmony back into our lives. Emma, poor thing, could sense the tension in the house between Ken and me. Despite being easy-going and a source of joy, she too was affected by the strain caused by Logan's demanding needs, which consumed much of my energy.

After the incident on Easter, Ken reluctantly agreed to let me take Logan to see Dr. Minton, the psychiatrist. Ken wasn't sure we should tell his parents. As soon as we entered the doctor's office, Logan immediately ran over and sat in the doctor's lap, embracing him tightly. It was almost too tight, and when I went to retrieve Logan, he clung to my neck so tightly that I could walk back to the chair without physically supporting him.

I showed Dr. Minton how Logan clung to me and explained his alternating desire for affection and hyperactivity. Dr. Minton noted that Logan had been excessively affectionate with him and inquired if that was a recurring pattern. I admitted that I never knew whom Logan would hug, whether it be the UPS man or the mail carrier. Exhausted from living with Logan, I looked directly at the doctor and uttered, "Medicate him or medicate me. I am toast." Dr. Minton proceeded to ask me numerous questions, and I divulged every detail that I could recall from the past year.

After about an hour, Logan grew bored and started wandering around the office. As I moved to intervene, Dr. Minton advised me to let him continue as he wanted to observe Logan. The doctor silently observed as Logan played. Eventually, Logan indicated that he was ready to leave. When I informed him that we were not finished, he reached over and pinched my arm. I pulled away and firmly stated, "No sir! We do not hurt mommy!" This agitated Logan, and he began kicking my legs. I tried to distract him by offering juice from a sippy cup, but he snatched it and threw it against the wall, causing a nearby vase to fall and shatter. In response, the doctor exclaimed, "STOP, Logan!" and managed to redirect him with a plastic robot. I told the doctor that I was having trouble bonding with Logan and explained I had no trouble bonding with Emma. I explained both children were adopted but it felt different with Logan.

Feeling helpless, I turned to Dr. Minton and pleaded for an explanation of what was wrong with Logan. He responded, saying, "It doesn't matter what you call it. No doctor will label or diagnose him until he reaches his teenage years." He explained that the available medication for very young children would remain the same regardless of the diagnosis. After weighing the pros and cons, Dr. Minton prescribed Risperdal to be taken twice a day. He explained that this medication would help calm Logan, allowing him to take naps, go to bed at night, and sleep. Dr. Minton emphasized that Risperdal had been effective in treating irritability and severe behavioral problems in children. He also expressed concern over tantrums and aggression starting at such a young age and requested that Ken and I return with Logan in two weeks for a follow-up session.

Logan left the doctor's office with a cherry sucker in his mouth, and I immediately called Ken to inform him about what the doctor had said. However, Ken insisted on keeping Logan's need for medication a secret, as his family had a strong sense of pride. While waiting for Logan's prescription to be filled, I approached the pharmacist and discreetly inquired about the drug's usage in adults. He whispered back that it was an antipsychotic medication commonly used to treat bipolar disorder and autism. This revelation felt like a slap to the face. No one knew for certain what was wrong with Logan, but I began to fear that it might be something more serious than just ADHD.

Dr. Minton requested that I keep a behavioral chart to monitor Logan's progress after starting the medication. The first night, he slept soundly, but I still woke up out of habit after a year of constant vigilance. I had developed the acute listening skills of a trained assassin, always on edge, waking up at the slightest noise and wondering if it was Logan. Initially, the medication seemed to be working well for about two weeks, but as our follow-up appointment with the doctor approached, Logan's behavior began to deteriorate.

One moment, Logan would be sweet to Emma, and I could give him a bath and play with him. But in the next moment, he would try to bite and push her. When the medication wore off, he became extremely hyperactive, running rampant throughout the house. On one occasion, I asked Logan to eat something, and he hurled the TV remote at my head, screaming, "I don't like you!"

He spat at me and continued screaming until his voice became hoarse.

Emma cherished the moments when Logan was asleep; it was our time together. We would lie on her bed, talking about her day, laughing, and playing games. One of our favorite games was "Velvet Hammer," where we pretended to lightly hammer each other's arms. If you let the hammer drop, you would be tickled. It was a precious time for Emma to be a little girl, and I would hold her tightly, thanking her for all her help. But her life had become challenging with the presence of her adopted brother. Her friends stopped coming over to play because of Logan, so she always had to go to their houses instead. The other mothers were reluctant to have their daughters around Logan due to his difficult behavior, which caused me great embarrassment.

Ken remained distant and offered little support, often finding excuses to be away at work. My social life came to a halt as I was constantly tied to Logan's needs. I felt isolated and began to question if this was somehow my fault.

The following months were consumed by Logan's doctor appointments and shuttling Emma to and from school. My mother would occasionally babysit Logan and Emma when she was in town, but only if Logan was already asleep. It was the only respite I had until we eventually hired a nanny. Finally, I mustered the courage to tell Ken, "I would let a stranger himself babysit Logan if I thought I could get an hour's break. I can't take it anymore, and I can't do this alone." Feeling horrible about saying that I apologized to Ken.

The nanny didn't last long and quit after just one month of dealing with Logan's behavior. One day, Jill came over to watch Logan while I ran errands. When I returned, I expressed my discouragement to Jill about how difficult it was to handle Logan. I couldn't help but feel anxious despite loving him so much. Logan's unpredictable nature kept me on edge, never knowing what he would do next. Jill agreed with my frustrations and suggested that I take him back to the doctor.

Finally, Ken and I met with Dr. Minton to review the behavioral logs I had kept for Logan. Ken had numerous questions and sought answers. However, Dr. Minton reiterated that Logan was too young for a definitive diagnosis and that we would have to experiment with different medications to see what worked. He decided to increase Logan's Risperdal dosage to four times a day and sent us on our way. It was disheartening to think that Logan was already on medication before even starting school, but I tried not to dwell on it.

On a Saturday, Forrest wanted to take Logan out for ice cream, so he made arrangements with Ken. I took Emma to her soccer game while Ken stayed home with Logan, wanting to impress his father by being actively involved with Logan's care. To ensure Logan would be calm, Ken gave him his Risperdal earlier than usual. Unfortunately, Logan fell asleep inside the ice cream shop, and Forrest had to carry him to the car. Logan slept throughout the entire car ride back home.

Forest was upset and confronted Ken, claiming that there was nothing wrong with Logan except for overmedication. This led to a heated argument by the time I arrived home. Ken demanded that we take Logan off his medication to see what would happen, so I called Dr. Minton for his opinion. Surprisingly, Dr. Minton agreed, stating that it might be worth observing the effects. Little did I know that he was well aware of what would happen to Logan once the medication left his system.

Within 24 hours of being off his medication, Logan had a screaming fit that lasted nearly an hour. He repeatedly screamed, "I hate you," at me until he was hoarse. Then he threw a glass of orange juice in Emma's hair, locked himself in the bathroom, and kicked the door with such force that it left dents in the wood. Frantically, I called Ken, begging him to come home and help. When Ken arrived, he swiftly grabbed Logan by the shirt, strapped him into the car seat, and drove to McDonald's so Logan could eat something. The change of environment seemed to help him calm down, and Logan eventually fell asleep in the car. After that incident, Ken decided to put Logan back on his medication, and I gained a newfound respect for Dr. Minton. It was the proof Ken needed to see that the medication helped stabilize Logan's mood.

Deep down, I knew that something was seriously wrong. The fear overwhelmed me, tightening the back of my neck. Logan's sudden bursts of energy and violent behavior troubled me deeply. The problem was that I didn't know how to confront this fear that lurked within me.

CHAPTER 11

In the midst of Logan's challenges, Ken became fixated on getting a new house. He desired a larger home with luxurious features like an outdoor kitchen, a full entertainment area by the pool, and glass walls that slid open for parties. Despite already living in an upscale neighborhood, Ken wanted to maintain and elevate our status, so we decided to stay in the same neighborhood and have a custom home built according to his desires. The distraction of the house construction offered some respite from Logan's issues.

Due to the high demand for homes in our area, we were able to sell our current house within just two days. Ken hired a company to handle the packing and moving, allowing me to focus on watching the kids. Although the new house was beautiful, I couldn't help but question if our lives would revolve around acquiring material possessions. There was always someone with a bigger house or a nicer car, and it felt like Ken was constantly trying to outdo them. He always sought the latest and greatest, yet never seemed content.

After we settled into the new home, Ken decided to throw a big party to celebrate. There were some final details that needed fixing before the event, so the house was filled with workers. During this time, I stayed home to ensure that everything on the punch list was addressed correctly. I dreaded Ken's anger; he was extremely meticulous and hard to please.

Ken wasn't satisfied with the wallpaper in the entry hall bath, so he hired a painter who specialized in faux-finishes to change it. Logan was running around the house and getting in the way, so I decided to take him to Chick-fil-A while the painter worked. As I was informing the painter that we were leaving, Logan unexpectedly ran in and punched him in the groin. The poor man doubled over in pain, making a horrible gasp. I apologized profusely, explaining that Logan was adopted and had some issues. In response, the painter stood up, looked me in the eye, and callously said, "Well, maybe his mother should have had an abortion." I left the house with tears streaming down my cheeks, my heart filled with pain for this child whose problems seemed to be mounting. It was a deeply hurtful thing for the painter to say.

The next few days in our house were challenging. Logan had found his way into the garage, climbed into Ken's beloved sedan, and colored all over the leather seats and console with an ink pen. Ken referred to the car as his "girlfriend" because he cherished it so much. When he discovered what Logan had done, he became furious and spanked Logan with a belt, leaving bruises on his behind. I was upset and disappointed that Ken had struck Logan out of anger. This child already had enough difficulties to face and did not need that type of punishment.

After that episode, Ken hired Vera, an ex-basketball player and coach, to be Logan's nanny. She was over six-feet-tall and had a very muscular build so she could handle Logan when he behaved badly. He did better when it was just him at home without many people around, so Vera home-schooled him when he was in a good mood.

One morning Emma came down ready for school and sat down to eat her oatmeal. She seemed very happy that morning and looked cute in her school uniform. We were chatting away about her day when suddenly Logan ran into the room with a white extension cord in his hand and began whipping Emma on the back with it. I immediately yelled at him to stop, but then he began hitting me with it. The weight of the plug on the end made this a real weapon.

When I grabbed the cord and jerked it out of Logan's hand, he bit me on the arm leaving deep teeth marks above my wrist. It really hurt. Then he took off running and knocked over a lamp. When I went after him, he turned and spit on me so I yelled, "No! No sir." This only made him laugh and he began pounding on my legs and stomach with his fists, all the while growling and making monster noises. Then he ran and climbed up the outside of the staircase screaming, "I don't like you." A short time later, he jumped off the stairs and sat down to watch TV and seemed much calmer.

After Logan went upstairs, I went to comfort Emma. She was crying and traumatized by the whole situation. Thankfully, Vera arrived at that moment. She could tell that we had had a bad morning with Logan by the look on my face. "Awful early for an episode," she said. I just shook my head which told it all. Logan's "episodes" marked our days. We just tried to live in between them, never knowing when he would have another one.

It was time to leave for school, so I wiped Emma's tears, picked up her lunch box and my purse and we walked to the garage. On the way to school, I kept telling her how much I loved her and how sorry I was that she had been hurt. Emma didn't seem that upset anymore by Logan's behavior. His episodes were becoming more frequent and she was growing accustomed to them. She and I bore the brunt of Logan's behavior. Ken was gone all the time, leaving early in the morning and not returning until late at night, so he only experienced an occasional episode on the weekend. My tolerance for discomfort was high and I am beyond my comfort zone with Logan. I am not sure what to do at this point.

On Logan's birthday, Ken invited his entire family over for a pool party. I cooked and we had a Batman-themed birthday cake. Logan, over-excited and very hyper, was running around dressed in his Batman suit making the cape fly behind him. He was having a great time and was fun to see him playing. Logan was pretending and he said Spiderman and Superman were flying with him. He had a vivid imagination.

When Evelyn, Forrest, and Maureen walked in, Jill whispered in my ear, "Dominating, Spoiled, and Neurotic have arrived." Robert was already there, and Travis was with the twins, Sam and Shelby. Then I heard Aunt Evil call out to Logan, "Come here, sweetheart. I want to take your picture." Logan rushed over and proudly declared, "I am not sweetheart, I am BATMAN!" After quickly posing for one picture, he darted off.

With the other kids eager to get in the pool, I helped Logan change his clothes in the kitchen. He was behind the counter, repeatedly saying, "Hurry! Hurry! Hurry!" as he wanted to be the first to jump in. Maureen and Forrest were sitting at the counter and could see Logan changing into his swimsuit. Maureen noticed the bruises on Logan's behind but didn't mention anything at that moment.

Soon, all the kids were joyfully splashing in the pool, accompanied by music from the faux rock speakers in the landscaping, and the LED lights illuminating the water with vibrant colors. It was a scene of pure enjoyment.

The adults sat around tables by the pool, observing the children's play. Out of the corner of my eye, I noticed Maureen and Evelyn cornering Ken, engrossed in a deep conversation. Then, they called Emma out of the pool and started examining her back. I moved closer and overheard them asking Emma about the bruises on her back. She revealed that Logan had hit her with an extension cord. Maureen, while looking at me, remarked to Ken, "It looks like my grandchildren have been abused." I firmly responded, "I refuse to dignify that accusation with a response." Evelyn interjected and called Forrest into the situation. Forest, who only seemed concerned about Logan, looked bored.

Evelyn demanded an explanation for what had happened to Emma. Just then, Logan emerged from the pool, his sagging bathing suit revealing the bruises on his behind. Evelyn became furious, unleashing a torrent of anger and threatening Armageddon. Ken remained silent, failing to come to my defense. Overwhelmed, I erupted, "Ken spanked Logan, not me!" Amidst the chaos, everyone began yelling and bombarding me with questions. I was devastated by Ken's refusal to speak up and convey the truth about Logan's struggles to his family. I had trusted him to defend me and shed light on what was really happening with Logan. Instead, he blamed me for spanking him, concealing the fact that he had bruised Logan over the ink in his car. This betrayal tore a hole in my heart. Ken was driving a wedge between us.

The situation felt utterly chaotic, suffocating me emotionally. Jill came out and stood by my side, offering protective support. I realized that fairness had been discarded as I witnessed the extent of Ken's unpredictability when it came to maintaining appearances in front of his family. The Burnett family had no idea about the immense challenges we faced in dealing with Logan.

Jill led me inside and solemnly said, "You are on your own when it comes to dealing with Logan's problems."

CHAPTER 12

I was at the end of my rope, completely overwhelmed by the challenges Logan had presented. Desperate for support, I called my mother in Charleston and burst into tears as soon as she answered. Through my sobs, I managed to convey, "I just can't handle this anymore!" I poured out the details of how difficult things had become with Logan and Ken. Mom listened patiently, offering a comforting presence, and then assured me that she would come over and stay for a week or two to help me and be there for me.

My mother, Suzanne Stenson, was a rational and compassionate woman. More than ever, I needed her sensible and warm personality. She had always been a source of stability, which was exactly what I needed at that moment.

When Mom arrived, we embraced with heartfelt hugs, and Ken graciously carried her bags upstairs to the guest room.

Coincidentally, Logan was in an affectionate mood that day and wanted me to hold him, so I cradled him in my arms as he hugged my neck. I expressed my deep gratitude to Mom for being there and how happy I was to have her support. She responded with a smile, stating that she was glad to do it, and then proceeded upstairs to take a bath and settle in. Emma was thrilled and eagerly anticipated going for a manicure with her Mimi.

While I was downstairs with the kids, a sudden deluge of water poured out of the vent in the dining room. I screamed for Ken to come, and fortunately, the water stopped after a short burst. Ken immediately became furious and called the builder, demanding that someone investigate the issue first thing in the morning. Ken had been meticulous about the construction of our house, even hiring an additional inspector to scrutinize the builder's work and ensure everything was fixed to perfection.

Earlier, Ken had already confronted the builder because water had seeped in through the French doors during a storm, causing damage to the wood floor in his office. The flashings around the doors had to be replaced, and Ken was livid about it. It was certainly not the ideal way for my mother's visit to commence.

The following morning, the builder dispatched a team of four men to determine the cause of the water issue. They discovered that the plumbing in the guest room had not been connected properly. When my mom unplugged the bathtub, the water flowed into the wall through a vent, eventually finding its way down to the dining room.

Ken responded to this incident by sending a harsh and strongly worded email to the builder, signing both our names. The builder expressed sincere apologies and swiftly worked to have the tub repaired within two days. While the workers were present, Mom oversaw their progress, while Vera attentively watched over Logan.

The next day, Mom took Emma out for ice cream after school, providing a much-needed break from the constant stress of Logan's behavior. During their outing, Emma casually mentioned, "Logan has HGTV." Mom, slightly confused, asked, "Don't you mean ADHD?" Emma corrected herself and continued to talk, sharing the story of a mean girl at school who wouldn't let their Barbies live together when they played. Mom chuckled, recognizing that it was beneficial for Emma to have a normal outing without the weight of Logan's challenges.

Observing my struggle to relax, Mom acknowledged that Jill was right. With Ken frequently angry about something and Logan being a constant source of chaos, my life lacked stability. I rarely found a moment to sit down, let alone unwind. While discussing their outing, Emma expressed her desire for more sprinkles on her ice cream. Mom complimented Emma on her pretty eyes and engaged her in conversation, providing the attention she craved. They even went shopping for headbands before returning home.

It didn't take long for Mom to notice the true state of affairs between Ken and me. Ken offered no assistance with the kids and neglected his responsibilities around the house. Witnessing my struggles while holding down a job and trying to manage Logan's behavior, Mom became frustrated. She understood that I was trapped in a war zone and felt powerless to help.

One night, after putting the kids to bed, Mom was upstairs when she overheard Ken berating me. Intrigued, she stopped at the top of the stairs and listened in.

Ken was unleashing his anger on me over the color of the grout. He accused me of purposefully changing it against his wishes. I tried to explain that I had nothing to do with the grout choice, but he was already angry and yelled, "I wanted the travertine to have a darker grout, and you knew that. Never do that again! Don't ever change something I want." Ken's outrage had made him completely unreasonable. I repeatedly insisted that I hadn't changed the color, explaining that the workers who laid the travertine had matched the grout accordingly.

Meanwhile, Mimi couldn't help but think out loud, "I would have told him to jump in a lake." She recognized that Ken never treated me this way when others were around. Being exposed to this side of Ken made her uneasy. She had a front-row seat in my life, and what she witnessed left her deeply dissatisfied.

The next morning, when Mom came downstairs, Ken had already left. She looked me directly in the eyes and said, "I heard Ken berating you last night. Just so you know, I would have told him to go jump in a lake."

"I felt humiliated," I confessed to my mother. "Mom, it's just easier not to argue with him. I can't win when he gets so angry about trivial things. Besides, I don't have the energy to fight after dealing with Logan all day." "Logan woke up screaming last night," my mother said.

"Yeah, he has night terrors and it happens quite often. Usually, he goes back to sleep or comes to get me. I hope it didn't keep you up for long," I replied, concerned about my mother's well-being.

My mother then inquired about Logan's upcoming doctor's appointment. I informed her that it was scheduled for two weeks from now. She expressed her concern, saying that Logan seemed to be getting worse, and asked, "Do you think he will outgrow this?"

"Sure, he will," I responded, trying to maintain a facade of positivity and pretend that everything was fine. Deep down, though, I knew the truth. Logan's condition was not improving, and it was becoming increasingly difficult to go out to restaurants as he couldn't sit still.

"Mom, the last time we went out with the Burnett family, Logan put three rocks in his pocket from the potted plants near the entrance. Once we were seated, he took out the stones and threw them across the room. One of them hit an elderly woman on the forehead, and her daughter came to our table and berated me. It was humiliating. Ken had me take Logan home in the car while Forest and Maureen drove him and Emma back after they finished their meal. Why did I have to leave with Logan? He has two parents," I lamented.

"Kate, when Ken demeans you in front of Emma, he is teaching her what level of respect to accept from the man she will marry one day," my mother said, her voice filled with concern.

Then my mother delved deeper, expressing an interest in how Ken treated me in the bedroom. I confided in her, sharing that Ken rarely showed any affection towards me and displayed no interest in satisfying my needs. In response, she suggested that I make an extra effort in that area to help salvage our marriage.

That remark crossed a line. "I have, mother. I've pleaded with Ken for us to see a counselor. But he told me that I was too fat to have sex with and he never touches me," I snapped, my frustration and hurt evident.

"Kate, no! You are beautiful. That is a ridiculous excuse," my mother reassured me.

Mom was right. I rested my head on her shoulder, letting out sobs of pent-up emotions. She held me tightly and rubbed my back, just like she did when I was little. Then she acknowledged the stress of raising Logan and the strain it had put on our family, acknowledging, "I am so sorry, sweet girl." My mother could see the toll my life had taken on me. The once-bright sparkle in my eyes had dimmed. My life felt chaotic as if the world was throwing sand in my eyes, making it hard to focus on what I truly wanted.

The following day, Mom took Emma shopping for clothes after school, bringing joy to Emma's face. When they returned home, Emma eagerly modeled the fancy new dress that Mimi had bought for her to wear to the Candlelight service at church on Christmas Eve. Mom suggested that we put up the Christmas tree early since she was there to help and thought it would lift my spirits. I thought it was a fantastic idea. Emma adored this part of our family tradition, and doing it together would be enjoyable.

Vera kindly offered to retrieve the plastic bins from the attic, so I put on a workout clip for Logan and me while we waited. It was an activity he enjoyed doing with me. We set up a tree in the playroom for Logan, allowing him to decorate it with superhero ornaments however he pleased. Then we placed a formal tree in the living room near the fireplace, positioning it so that the lights would be visible from the street. Christmas was the most cherished holiday for me, and putting up the trees helped elevate my mood. I loved Christmas and took pleasure in wrapping gifts with matching paper, adding to the festive ambiance. It was truly my favorite time of year, and I had a passion for decorating in shades of red, my favorite color.

The next day at work, Forrest invited Ken and me to have lunch with him. He wanted to discuss something he had heard on the golf course. Once we were seated, Forrest confronted us about the scathing emails that were sent to the builder regarding the house. He informed us that the builder had been sharing his troubles with other people at the club, claiming that he had never encountered such difficulties with a client before. Ken immediately became defensive, blaming the builder and the foreman for the issues and insisting that everything in the emails was true. He also mentioned that I had drafted the letter and that my anger had influenced the tone, adding that my mother agreed with me.

I was dumbfounded, nearly falling out of my chair. I had never seen Ken lie so effortlessly. He made it sound so convincing, spewing lies without even a hint of truth. I hadn't even seen the email.

Forrest cautioned us against putting anything in writing without being absolutely sure of what we were doing. He emphasized the importance of not attacking people in the community and associating the Burnett name with such actions, as it reflected poorly on him. He directed his comments toward me since Ken had blamed me for the incident.

When Ken and I returned to work, he acted as if nothing had happened. I couldn't believe how he could separate himself so easily. We didn't even discuss it. I was slowly becoming a doormat wife, feeling increasingly powerless.

Feeling mentally drained after the encounter, I used the excuse of needing to check on Logan and went home. When I arrived, Logan had just finished an episode where he had locked himself in Ken's office and used a paperweight to bang on the door. Vera was worried that Ken would be angry about the marks left on the door. I reassured Vera and told her to go home. I couldn't help but notice how worn out she looked, despite her strong, six-foot- tall frame.

Mom prepared dinner and was feeding the kids when Ken arrived home. He greeted the children with his usual hugs and kisses, showering them with affection. My mother had been there long enough to notice that Ken never hugged me when he arrived. After the kids finished eating, they went to the playroom while we had our dinner. Ken then left again to attend the Homeowners' Association Board meeting.

I told my mom that I felt like something was up with Ken. Little did I know that the drama about to unfold would turn my life completely inside out. Mom told me that she had read a quote somewhere that said, "Spend your time on those people who love you unconditionally, and don't waste it on those who only love you when the conditions are right for them." That comment really made me think. Then Mom said very gently, "I don't like the way he treats you Kate. He doesn't even hug you or speak to you when he comes home." I told her that I didn't know what to do. Ken and I disagree about Logan's care and he blamed me for the bad behavior. Ken would not accept that Logan had a medical condition so he refused to deal with it. My life was not how she imagined it. Mom had concern in her eyes.

Ken was nice to me when people were around, which made me want to always have company. I dreaded being alone with him because he was so critical of me. Mom took me in her arms and held me for a long time. Then she said, "I am always here for you baby; you just have to make the best of it for Emma." Mom encouraged me to spend time with my girlfriends and take care of myself.

My mother's visit came to an end and now I had to decide what to do about Logan. Wearily, I made an appointment with the head of the best child and adolescent psychiatrist for a complete evaluation. It was time to bring in the big guns.

CHAPTER 13

Ken struggled to accept the reality of Logan's mental and behavioral disorders, which led him to believe that he needed a break. Without much consultation, he arranged to attend a nine-day conference in California. Although he had already made the travel arrangements, I agreed that the trip could be beneficial for him, hoping that he might gain some valuable insights. Honestly, I also needed a break from him. They say absence makes the heart grow fonder, right?

During one of the nights when Ken was away, I was abruptly awakened by Logan's presence next to my bed. Startled, I noticed that he was completely naked and had used a blue sharpie marker to color his skin. It must have taken him hours to cover his chest and genitals so extensively. He had even drawn a mask on his face and a blue sleeve down his arm. It was as if he had outdone a professional tattoo artist. I exclaimed, "Holy crap, Batman … what have you done?" One of his legs was entirely colored royal blue, as were the tops of both his feet. I checked the soles of his feet, half-expecting to find blue sharpie footprints all over the house. Fortunately, they were untouched. Captivated by the absurdity of the situation, I couldn't help but laugh while taking pictures of Logan, who was beaming with pride.

Not knowing what else to do at 3 AM, I ran a bath and added bubbles. I pointed to the tub and said, "To the bathtub, Batman!" I quickly put on a bathing suit and knelt beside the tub once Logan got in. The marker had dried, and Logan was now a "permanently" tattooed superhero, half-covered in blue ink. Despite the situation, he was in a great mood. Removing the marker was futile, as it had stained his fair skin. Then I noticed his hair—Logan had colored a section above his ear to resemble a fender over a wheel. This sight sent me into another fit of laughter, and Logan joined in with giggles. He would place his Hulk action figure on the side of the tub, and I would playfully say, "You talking to me? NO!" while pushing it into the bubbles. Logan would repeatedly put the Hulk back on the tub's edge, and each time, he would burst into laughter, his eyes closed and mouth wide open. It was a story I would reminisce about countless times. That moment with Logan was a much-needed and enjoyable time for both of us. He stayed in the tub until the water turned cold, and then we drained some and added more warm water.

Amidst the constant fear I experienced, it was refreshing to have moments like these with Logan. The following morning, Emma squealed with laughter when Logan proudly showed off his new blue superhero costume. The ink had stubbornly clung to his skin, seemingly impervious even to gasoline. It would simply have to wear off over time. Meanwhile, Emma kept her bedroom door locked at night because I didn't feel she was safe. Logan lacked the ability to handle his emotions appropriately, and it seemed to amuse him to witness my fear, making him laugh at my expense. Parenting a violent, abusive, uncontrollable, hyperactive child was incredibly challenging. I loved him, yet I also feared him and he knew it. To protect myself, I had learned to conceal my emotions from Logan.

The following day was a Saturday, and Emma had a birthday party to attend. After dropping her off, Logan and I headed home, with Logan engrossed in a handheld game. When we arrived at our destination and parked the car, Logan refused to get out because he hadn't finished playing. Frustrated, I decided to leave him in the car and walked away. Glancing back, I saw him unleashing his anger by punching and kicking the seats. Concerned, I returned and opened all the car doors, starting a chase with him. He leaped from the front seat to the back as I attempted to grab his arm or catch hold of his shirt. Eventually, I managed to grasp his shirt, but he promptly took it off. Worried he might bolt, knowing he was a fast runner, I called out to him, "Logan, get out of the car."

Finally, I managed to secure a grip on his upper arm and led him outside, placing him by the car. He resumed playing with his handheld game as I locked the car doors. Suddenly, as if a switch had been flipped, he climbed onto the roof of the car and began jumping on it like a trampoline. He repeatedly slammed his butt down, stood up, and jumped down again, causing the roof to dent and cave in. Despite my desperate pleas for him to stop, he persisted. As the roof continued to bow and cave, I frantically reached for my cell phone and dialed my friend Maggie.

Maggie promptly contacted her husband Mark, who was a tall, strong man. He arrived to help, standing on one side of the car while I positioned myself on the other. Mark managed to catch hold of Logan by the foot and then secured him underneath the armpits. I grabbed his feet, and together we carried him towards the house, with Logan screaming and kicking throughout the ordeal. He even bit Mark's hand and arm, causing Mark to flip him over his shoulder. However, Logan persisted, biting Mark on the back and pounding him with his fists.

Once we reached the front door, Mark released his grip on Logan, who immediately seized a bar stool and began swinging it as a weapon. He threw the bar stool, narrowly missing the large plate- glass wall. Reacting swiftly, Mark grabbed hold of Logan again and pinned him down while I hurried to retrieve a sedative that could dissolve in his mouth. It was essential to calm him down. Despite Logan's continuous yelling, biting, and spitting, I managed to place the tablet in his open mouth with Mark's assistance, as the doctor had suggested.

Logan's breathing gradually started to slow down, so we sat him up and backed away cautiously. In an instant, he reached for his next makeshift weapon, my coin bag, and started hurling change at me. Mark shouted, "What do I do?" Logan began hitting me with the silk bag, causing a stinging sensation on my leg. Mark swiftly took the coin bag away, further agitating Logan, who retaliated by grabbing a handful of my hair and pulling me to the ground. I found myself pinned to the floor by a six-year-old boy! In the midst of our struggle, Logan kicked me in the ribs, sending waves of pain through my body. Together, Mark and I managed to secure Logan in a protective hold, doing our best to prevent him from harming himself or either of us.

Both of us were drenched in sweat as Mark pried Logan off of me. Exhausted, I went limp, and once again, Logan's demeanor shifted, and he started engrossing himself in his iPad. I expressed gratitude to Mark, assuring him that everything was under control and that Logan had endured worse episodes before.

Horrified, Mark stared at me and voiced his concern, "You can't handle this child. I'm a big guy, and he was a handful for me. This isn't going to work, and why is he covered in blue?"

In that moment, reality began to sink in. Mark was right. I couldn't continue like this. It was only a matter of time before Logan would harm me. I shuddered at the thought of what might have happened if Emma had been present.

I reached out to Vera and implored her to stay with me until Ken returned, promising her any compensation she desired. The prospect of being alone with Logan was something I dreaded. Vera, with her strong hands, handled Logan better than I ever could. She was a true blessing, and I couldn't have coped without her.

"Do you want me to tie him up?" Vera joked.

I forced a sarcastic smile and shook my head, although there were moments when I genuinely wondered. Logan's behavior seemed to be growing increasingly peculiar and violent with each passing day.

After regaining some composure, I dialed Ken in California and recounted what had transpired. I desperately wanted him to cut his conference short and come home, but he insisted on calling Mark to ascertain the severity of the situation.

An hour later, Ken called me back, revealing his decision not to return. Instead, he instructed me to contact Logan's behavioral counselor, Pam, and apprise her of the incident. I promptly called Pam and arranged an emergency session for the following day.

Pam arrived at the house the next morning, prepared to observe Logan for an entire day. We meticulously reviewed his medication schedule and daily routine, as Pam sought to understand the dynamics between Vera and Logan. Once the necessary updates were addressed, she settled into the playroom to observe him.

After dropping off Emma at school, I met Jo Ann for a much-needed coffee break. I shared with her the distressing episode involving Logan. Hearing the details, she remarked, "That is not normal behavior. No one acts like that. Was his birth mother struggling with drug addiction or mental illness?"

I confided in Jo Ann, admitting that I had pondered the same questions. She then raised the possibility of Logan having Asperger's or Autism. I explained that I had extensively researched the conditions. I mentioned that the adoption agency had assured us of Logan's good health, yet it was evident that something was amiss. Jo Ann expressed deep concern for my well-being and feared that someone would eventually get hurt. I refrained from disclosing the extent of Logan's violence, like the forceful kick to my ribs that knocked the wind out of me. I felt utterly humiliated by my adopted son's behavior.

Regrettably, our time together with Jo Ann had to come to an end. I embraced her in a hug and informed her that I needed to return home since Pam was still observing Logan. Upon my arrival, I was met with the piercing screams of Logan, who had broken a vase by forcefully striking it against the master bedroom door. "Here we go again," I sighed.

Vera quickly briefed me on the recent events. Waving her large hands in the air, she recounted, "Logan poured a glass of orange juice on the floor because he refused to eat at the table, and then he threw a framed picture. Pam attempted various techniques to calm him down."

As Logan darted by, screaming at the top of his lungs, I swiftly caught hold of him. However, in his frenzy, he bit my hand, pinched my arm, and began striking me. Pam advised me to restrain him in a hold, but Logan managed to break free and barricaded himself in the bathroom. He repeatedly slammed the toilet seat while bellowing, "I hate you," his voice already strained from prolonged screaming.

Resting on the back of the toilet was a decorative wooden box that Logan seized and hurled against the glass shower door. Then, he flung it forcefully at the back of the bathroom door.

Vera promptly contacted the doctor, who advised, "Administer the Risperdal and a Klonopin, and if he doesn't calm down soon, take him to the emergency room." I stressed that we couldn't possibly get him into a car and drive, fearing that he would harm us all. The doctor instructed us to call 911 if necessary.

I continued to engage with Logan after concluding the call, as an eerie silence settled within the bathroom. Vera attempted to pick the lock, but Logan cunningly held the button in, a trick he had already mastered. He was remarkably intelligent.

Finally, Logan muttered, "Mommy, I'm thirsty," and emerged from the bathroom, seeking solace in my embrace. He displayed immense affection and hugged my neck tightly. After a grueling thirty-five-minute tantrum, he had transformed from a wild creature into a loving child.

Vera brought Logan some juice, and I sat there, cradling him in my arms. Pam informed us that she would return the next day, and I informed her that around six p.m. was the dreaded "witching hour" when Logan's behavior tended to escalate.

When Pam arrived the following evening, Logan was in a foul mood. I switched off the television, which immediately angered him, leading to him pinching my face. He proceeded to spit on me and demand, "Turn it on." In an attempt to regain control, I restrained him, but he retaliated by biting both of my hands, causing a blood-blister to form from the intensity of the bite. With Logan seated in front of me, I tightly held onto him. At that moment, I shouted at Emma to retreat to her room. Suddenly, Logan forcefully lunged backward, using the back of his head to head-butt me. The impact was painful, bringing tears to my eyes, and he callously uttered, "I don't like you." Drawing closer, Pam tried to reason with Logan, promising to release him if he calmed down. Instead, Logan spat on her, managed to free one of his arms, and struck her in the face, causing her glasses to fall off. He responded to the situation with laughter.

After approximately ten minutes, Logan began to calm down, allowing me to release my grip on him. Expressing his desire to watch TV, Pam granted him permission. We seized this opportunity for Pam to peruse my journals documenting Logan's behavior. Hearing her read my words aloud felt surreal:

Monday, April 8: Logan hit Emma and attempted to bite her, even trying to knock her down while she was putting on her rollerblades. However, he later displayed a sweet and affectionate demeanor, engaging in playful activities with her.

Tuesday, April 9: Logan expressed extreme fear of sleeping in his room, convinced that bugs were present in his air vents. This worries me greatly. I contemplate his future, concerned that he might harm me during the night. Despite these difficulties, I truly love him and want him to be okay. I also consider providing a separate apartment above the garage for the nanny, allowing Logan to spend two nights a week with her so that I can get some sleep.

Wednesday, April 10: Logan threw orange juice on Emma's school books while declaring, "I don't like you, stupid. I hate you." He slammed doors, broke his Spiderman fishing pole in half, spat at me, and overturned the leather chair. He refused to cease running and continuously circled the house.

Thursday, April 11: Logan appeared agitated, repeatedly stating, "I need to hit someone." He claimed that lizards were present in his room, urging me to check beneath the bed. To my astonishment, I discovered five red solo cups filled with urine neatly lined up in a row.

Friday, April 12: Logan reiterated his belief that bugs had infested his room through the air vents. In frustration over receiving an insufficient portion of ice cream, he hurled a bowl across the room, shattering it.

Pam inquired if I had documented everything, to which I admitted that I lacked the time and only managed to jot down one episode per day. Even that was a challenging task.

Pam remarked, "His violence and behavior, frequent outbursts of anger, and tantrums are concerning. I'm particularly troubled by his cruelty towards the dog." Pam explained that while observing Logan watch TV, our dog Skipper had been lying next to him. Unexpectedly, Logan grabbed Skipper's paw and forcefully pulled it apart, causing the poor dog to cry out in pain. Logan then proceeded to restrain Skipper, sitting on him until the frightened dog urinated on the floor.

I felt stunned and remorseful for our gentle little King Charles Cavalier Spaniel. Ken had paid a considerable sum for that puppy. Now, I had to ensure Skipper's safety from Logan as well. It was all too overwhelming. I loved that dog. There was clearly more at play here than met the eye. I questioned Pam about Logan's condition, and she responded, "It's too early to say, but I've encountered children like him before. Usually, it's a result of their birth mothers using drugs during pregnancy." She continued, "Logan is still young, and most psychiatrists won't provide a diagnosis until he reaches his teens. Given his destructive, dangerous, and violent behavior, we should brace ourselves for it to worsen as he grows older." She also advised that we needed to find a suitable home for Skipper immediately.

Pam contacted Ken in California to update him about the dog, while I reached out to friends whom I thought could help. When I called my friend Belinda and inquired if she was still interested in a "King Charles," she expressed her enthusiasm to have him. Many people in our neighborhood desired that breed. As Emma and I took Skipper to Belinda's house, she warmly embraced Emma and assured her that she could visit Skipper anytime. On our way back home, I expressed my deep regret to Emma about what had happened to Skipper. She then confided in me that Logan had choked the dog a few days prior. Emma felt sorry for Skipper. Despite her young age, she possessed wisdom beyond her years. She understood that Logan was very ill, and she recognized the immense strain I was under.

Upon Ken's return from California, he swiftly realized that I desperately needed a break. He acknowledged, "I don't know what to do about Logan. Let's take a short trip together to see if we can gain some clarity. Emma can stay with Jill and the twins, and Vera can stay here with Logan. He tends to do better when he has one-on-one attention and no one else is around." I agreed wholeheartedly. It was true that Logan's behavior tended to improve when there were fewer people present. Ken suggested that we attend the Kentucky Derby since it had always been a dream of mine. He also proposed inviting Mark and Maggie, turning it into a weekend getaway. Ken wanted to do something nice for Mark as a gesture of gratitude for his help during one of Logan's outbursts.

Though exhausted, I felt a sense of relief that Ken was finally acknowledging that Logan was beyond our capabilities. It was evident that he was grappling with a severe mental illness, and we were ill-equipped to handle it.

CHAPTER 14

In preparation for our weekend getaway, Maggie and I ventured out to purchase large hats adorned with bows, indulging in a delightful time trying on various styles. It proved to be a stress-relieving experience as we eagerly anticipated the enjoyment that awaited us at the Kentucky Derby alongside our friends.

Ken approached Vera with an intriguing proposal, offering to trade her van for a newer and safer car in exchange for her looking after Logan during the weekend. Recognizing the need for an upgrade from her older model, Vera agreed to the arrangement. Ken promptly arranged for the dealership to deliver the new vehicle, though his true motivation stemmed from his weariness of the old van occupying the driveway. Meanwhile, we made arrangements for Emma to stay with her Aunt Jill while we were away.

Embarking on our journey, we boarded a business-class flight to Louisville and proceeded directly to the prestigious Galt House Hotel. Despite all rooms being fully booked, Ken managed to secure two suites boasting waterfront balconies. Notably, the Galt House stands as the largest hotel in Kentucky and serves as the official Derby hotel.

After settling into our accommodations, we ventured to the hotel's magnificent conservatory, an impressive glass-domed space reminiscent of London's Crystal Palace. Enveloped by lush tropical plants and the melodious presence of birds, we delighted in the ambiance for over an hour while relishing appetizers and engaging in conversations about our respective "bucket lists." Naturally, attending the Kentucky Derby had long been an item on my list, and I eagerly awaited hearing Mark and Maggie's aspirations.

Considering Mark's commendable progress in Alcoholics Anonymous, Maggie and I thoughtfully ordered sweet tea to ensure his comfort during our gathering. Ken opted for a glass of wine, and Mark assured us that we were free to enjoy a drink if we wished. On that particular day, Ken exhibited kindness toward me, and a wave of happiness enveloped me, fostering a sense of well-being.

When the topic of our aspirations arose, I enthusiastically shared my desire to charter a yacht and sail along the Italian Riviera. Maggie, on the other hand, expressed an interest in learning the art of stained glass. Amused by her choice, I chuckled and playfully exclaimed, "Stained glass? No way!"

During Ken's brief absence from the table, he returned with an exhilarated air. He had managed to acquire tickets to THE Kentucky Derby Party, an exclusive affair hosting renowned celebrities. With tickets priced at $1,650 per person, attending became an absolute must for us.

The hotel graciously arranged for a chauffeur to transport us, adding a touch of exclusivity to our experience. Upon arrival, we found ourselves amidst a sea of notable figures, including Celine Dion, Kevin Costner, as well as Faith Hill, and Tim McGraw. The sheer number of attendees made it quite challenging to secure seating. The event exuded elegance, adhering to a black-tie dress code. Having not experienced such relaxation and enjoyment with Ken for an extended period, I reveled in the lively atmosphere he orchestrated when he assumed the role of planner in the presence of others.

Saturday brought us to Churchill Downs, where we settled into our seats at the esteemed Turf Club. Arriving early granted us the opportunity to explore the revered track and capture cherished photographs.

After traversing the track, we made our way to the bustling paddock, filled to the brim with enthusiastic horse racing fans eagerly observing the horses and their jockeys. Maggie and I were captivated by the abundant display of blooming red roses and the splendidly manicured landscape. The paddock proved to be an excellent vantage point for people-watching, showcasing elegantly attired women and eccentrically dressed gentlemen sporting magnificent hats. Maggie commented on how this grand gesture exemplified Ken's signature style, always striving to surpass others. He often stated, "Go big or go home," and his actions certainly lived up to that motto.

Subsequently, we proceeded to the betting windows, placing our wagers. Maggie and I based our choices on the horses' names and the colors of the jockeys' attire. Our seats in the Turf Club afforded us an excellent view, and the private restrooms provided added convenience. Curiosity led us to the sky terrace in hopes of catching a glimpse of another celebrity. Ken, true to the occasion, ordered a Mint Julep, which I found rather distasteful; Maggie likened its flavor to mouthwash. As the trumpets began to resonate throughout the grounds, our focus shifted from the victor or potential Triple Crown recipient to the pure enjoyment of the betting experience.

Within the "members only" Turf Club, we were assigned a table for four. As the race commenced following the heartwarming rendition of "My Old Kentucky Home," the horses burst forth like lightning, and the crowd's roar filled the air, overwhelming our senses. Maggie's chosen horse briefly took the lead, eliciting her jubilant cries, "That's my horse, that's my horse!" However, in the final moments, another contender seized victory. It was an exhilarating two minutes, etching an indelible memory as the most remarkable sporting moment for us.

Alas, our cherished time away drew to a close all too quickly. As our plane descended toward home, a wave of anxiety washed over me. Reality was swiftly approaching, and I pondered how Logan had fared during our absence. Vera's report provided relief, assuring us that he had a pleasant weekend engaged in playing video games.

"Who does that?" Jo Ann exclaimed, referring to the unconventional family photo on our card taken inside Cinderella's Coach at Disney World. I couldn't help but respond, "Ken does. He will do whatever it takes to show off."

I recounted to Jo Ann the story of our first year of marriage when Ken discovered my fondness for Johann Sebastian Bach. Most husbands would have simply bought a CD or loaded the music onto their wife's phones, but not Ken. He whisked me away to Leipzig, Germany, where he took me to St. Thomas Church, the very place where Bach served as the choirmaster. To top it off, there was even a museum dedicated to Bach inside the church.

Jo Ann shared that during lunch the previous Sunday, everyone was discussing our Kentucky Derby trip and wondered what Ken had planned. With ample time on his hands, Ken had become quite the master of orchestrating grand excursions. He was always holed up in his home office with his laptop, and he kept it all secretive, not allowing me to see what he was up to or even pick up the mail. His phone and computer were off-limits to me, all in the name of preserving surprises.

As our pedicures dried, I suddenly noticed a missed call from Vera. Little did I know how that call would soon turn my world upside down.

When Emma and I arrived home, we were greeted by Logan in the midst of a full-blown attack. Vera had reached out to Ken for help, but she couldn't get through to him. So she had called Maureen instead. Ken had instructed Vera to stop all of Logan's medications while we were away, attributing his behavior solely to side effects. The detox had triggered an episode leaving Logan in a frenzied state of constant motion, uttering nonsensical words.

Logan's aggression escalated as he tried to rip Maureen's necklace off, then resorted to choking her. Vera managed to pull him away, but he broke free and began hitting his own arm, threatening to break it. Fearing for their safety, Maureen dialed 911, desperately requesting an ambulance for our dire situation.

Breathless and shaken, Vera explained, "Ken made me take him off all meds. He was sure it was the meds making him act badly, that it was all side effects." Time seemed to slow down as panic engulfed me. Logan's agitation and erratic behavior surpassed anything we had previously witnessed.

I instructed Emma to retreat to her room, lock the door, and put on her headphones. Logan darted into the bathroom and slammed the door shut. Finally, Ken arrived, and Maureen tried to update him on the ordeal. She was nearly hysterical as she recounted the bathroom door being locked, the toilet lid cover shattered on the tiled floor, holes punched in the drywall, choking and hitting, and Logan's threats to break his own arm. He had become a walking powder keg, emitting ear-piercing screams, hurling a handheld weight across the room, scratching, punching, yelling, and biting before running back to the bathroom, where he proceeded to tear the toilet paper roll off the wall and break the toilet lid in half.

This was a side of Logan that Maureen had never witnessed before—a full-blown episode of violence and destruction. I, too, had never seen him in this state, tearing apart our home and proving nearly impossible to handle.

Finally, the ambulance arrived. Logan continued to bite, spit, and hit the paramedics, necessitating that he be strapped onto a backboard and sedated with a shot. It was difficult to believe that this uncontrollable whirlwind of rage was only seven years old.

Vera remained shaken, her words tumbling out incoherently, "One minute sweet and loving, then it was like a switch was flipped, and Logan would attack. Then it would turn off again."

Ken and I trailed the ambulance to the hospital in our car. Logan was admitted and later transferred to Atlanta, where he spent two weeks as an inpatient in the children's psychiatric ward at Peachtree Hospital. Due to his threat of jumping out of a window, he was eventually moved to another specialized treatment unit for children. It was there that doctors diagnosed him as having autism spectrum disorder and possibly some kind of fetal alcohol syndrome.

My search for Logan's birth mother and Emily Searcy began, hoping to gain insight into the factors contributing to his behavior. I tracked down Logan's grandparents phone number and demanded immediate information about the birth mother Emily's mental health or substance abuse issues. I explained the urgency, emphasizing Logan's illness and the need for medical information. The grandmother revealed that Emily had come to live with them at fifteen due to her own mother's mental instability. She stayed for three years and became pregnant. Emily had a history of drug use and alcohol consumption, possibly during her pregnancy. Although she didn't want the baby, it was too late for an abortion.

I probed further, inquiring about the formal diagnosis of Emily's mother and her current whereabouts. The grandmother disclosed that her mother was living with mental illness refusing any form of treatment. She said maybe it was schizophrenia. The Searcey's were very guarded about the information they passed to me and said that Emily was missing. They said they needed to get off the phone.

My anger flared. I would have never adopted Logan had we known the truth, as schizophrenia has a hereditary component. The grandmother had broken down in tears, expressing her hope that Logan had not inherited the same condition. She added that he cried incessantly as a newborn and could never sleep for more than four hours at a time. Logan's grandparents were unable to care for them, leading to Logan's adoption. Forest had helped pay their bills according to the Searcy's. There was something that they were not telling me. What was going on?

As I processed this devastating information to me, I felt a mixture of sickness and panic. Our once-rosy future was now clouded with uncertainty. This problem was far larger than we ever anticipated, and we found ourselves at a loss for what to do next. Fear gripped me, not only for Emma but also for myself. What lies ahead for us?

Evelyn suggested that Logan be admitted to The Children's Hospital, renowned for its expert child psychiatrists. Ken and his parents made arrangements to travel there, while I stayed home with Emma, providing Vera with some well-deserved respite.

Logan was admitted to the Behavioral Center and placed in a ward with other children battling mental illness. He fit the criteria with a family history of drug use during pregnancy, and violent outbursts, including making threats to harm others. Forrest was slow to admit anything was wrong with Logan and expected him to grow out of it.

Slowly but surely, the puzzle pieces fell into place as we absorbed the doctors' explanations. Logan's self-talk and isolation from reality began to make sense. It was as if he inhabited his own insular world, shut off from the rest of us.

In the hospital, Logan grew increasingly unsettled, feeling as though someone was constantly watching him. He despised being confined there, and his irritability, rapidly shifting moods, and daily bursts of anger only intensified. His language, which we had brushed off as childish imagination, now seemed like part of a larger problem. He often regressed, acting much younger than his age, seeking constant comfort and even screaming at the TV to "shut up." Logan's behavior, once baffling, now aligned with the symptoms of his being on the spectrum.

This provided an explanation for his extreme mood swings, irritability, confusion, and agitation. It clarified the sudden outbursts triggered by seemingly insignificant noises in the environment. The psychiatrists also attributed his rage attacks to his birth mother's substance abuse during pregnancy.

CHAPTER 15

After Logan's discharge from the hospital, we enlisted the help of an orderly named Thomas to assist us during the day, while Vera supported us during the night.

Logan's transition back home was exceedingly challenging. In the initial days, his behavior escalated dramatically. He destroyed a dining room chair, hurled the video game, inflicted harm by punching Emma in the stomach, pinching my arm, and kicking my shin. During one particularly intense episode lasting an hour, he repetitively uttered the words, "I hate you." His actions became uncontrollable, and his erratic sleep pattern kept him awake at midnight, 2:00 a.m., and 4:30 a.m. On one occasion, he entered our room expressing a desire for a milkshake, followed by questioning the darkness enveloping us.

Emma, burdened by immense stress at this point, became the target of Logan's disruptive and hyperactive behavior, which made it increasingly challenging for her. One time he grew angry with her, and resorted to urinating in her dresser drawers.

During the nighttime, Logan would engage in destructive activities. One night, he used Liquid Paper white-out to deface the back of Ken's dark mahogany office door. His moods fluctuated wildly, making it exceedingly difficult to be around him. Some nights, we would abruptly awaken to blood-curdling screams, making every day an arduous struggle.

Logan's medication regimen had become exorbitant, bordering on absurd. Risperdal, Concerta, Trileptal, and Klonopin constituted his medication cocktail. At times, a chilling look of hatred in his eyes would send shivers down my spine, while other times he exhibited affection and kindness.

One night, Logan remained awake at 3:00 a.m., unable to fall back asleep. Vera stayed up with him and tried to engage him by putting on a movie. However, his exuberance disrupted the entire household, awakening everyone.

When I went to check on Vera, I picked up Logan, and to my dismay, he spit in my hair. His actions escalated as he began screaming, rushing into the garage, and seizing a hand-held weight to hurl it at the door. In an attempt to redirect him, Vera handed him a juice box, but as I turned around to enter the house, Logan struck me forcefully in the back with the corner of the juice box. The pain elicited a moan, which only provoked laughter from him. He then scratched Vera and hurled insults at her. In an alarming display, he clenched his teeth and let out a guttural yell.

Regrettably, Thomas proved unable to cope with the challenges and resigned, citing his unfamiliarity with such extreme agitation in a patient. Due to the concern for Emma's safety, the psychiatrist's office referred us to Nayda Parker, a social worker, to conduct an evaluation of Logan.

Upon Nadya's arrival, she expressed a desire to observe Logan during dinner. I informed her that Logan refused to sit at the table and instead ate in front of the television. That evening, Logan requested macaroni and cheese, and I prepared a bowl for him while he watched a movie.

Nayda inquired about Logan's daily activities, prompting me to explain the need for constant vigilance as he had a tendency to engage in mischievous behavior. I recounted the incident where he took a magic marker during the night and covered his entire body in blue ink.

Once Logan finished his dinner, Nayda expressed a desire to witness his bath and bedtime routine. Aware of the potential challenges she would face, I questioned her certainty in proceeding. She emphasized that her objective was to ensure we could provide Logan with basic care while safeguarding Emma.

That evening, with Ken and Emma out shopping and Vera off duty due to the presence of two adults in the house, I initiated Logan's bath by running the water. Upon entering the bathroom, I informed Logan that it was time for him to bathe, to which he objected, specifically resisting hair washing. As I insisted on washing his hair, his anger intensified. Reluctantly, he stepped into the tub but immediately began kicking and splashing water all over the bathroom. I raised my voice, attempting to halt his disruptive behavior, but he continued for a grueling fifteen minutes. By the time he ceased, I was drenched, my makeup smeared, and the bathroom floor was soaked.

Nayda's eyes widened in disbelief as she exclaimed, "Take hold of his upper arm and pull him out. I'm concerned he might harm himself in the tub."

Adhering to her instructions, I promptly removed Logan from the tub, his body dripping with water. As I turned to fetch a towel, he seized my hair, entwining it around his hand and forming a fist. With a powerful yank, he pulled me to the floor, my head pinned beneath him. A full-fledged struggle ensued, and I cried out for Nayda's assistance. However, she declined, citing her inability to physically intervene with a child.

My head pressed against the cold tile, tears streaming down my face as Logan continued to grasp my hair tightly. Suddenly, he sunk his teeth into my arm. Desperately, I jerked my arm free to break his grip, inadvertently striking him in the testicles. As he released my hair, I swiftly rose to my feet, observing a clump of my hair still clenched in his hand. Hurriedly, I wrapped him in a towel, picked him up, and placed him in front of the TV, all the while clutching the extended strand of hair. I informed Nayda that he had never exerted such force on my hair before. She noticed blood trickling from my scalp and fetched a paper towel to apply pressure to the wound.

Inquiring about the usual difficulty during bath time, Nayda sought clarification. I conveyed that Logan consistently splashed water in such a manner. Concerned, she mentioned the need to consult her supervisor and stepped outside onto the front porch. While she made the call, I checked on Logan, changed into a dry shirt, secured my wet hair with a clip, and wiped away the streaks of black mascara. My scalp throbbed with soreness, and a blood blister adorned my arm where he had bitten me.

Nayda reentered the room and stated, "I checked with my supervisor, and I don't have to report this as sexual abuse."

Anger coursed through me, and I demanded an explanation from Nayda. "What are you talking about? It was an accident. He was hurting me. You saw the whole incident," I retorted.

Nayda responded, "I am just doing my job. I have never experienced anything like this."

Just then, Logan walked in, holding a box of Kleenex. He handed me a tissue, climbed onto my lap, and hugged me affectionately. Nayda continued taking notes and informed me that she would write a report to send to Logan's psychiatrist. She also advised me to take Logan to see the doctor the following morning. Ken and Emma entered the room as Nayda left, so she quickly briefed Ken while I took Emma upstairs to bed.

When we took Logan to see the psychiatrist in Atlanta, the doctor determined that he needed to be readmitted to the hospital. After a week of observation, the medical team called for a conference to discuss Logan's illness. The lead psychiatrist offered to have additional family members present, signaling that they had troubling news. Ken contacted Forrest and Maureen, asking them to join us. My mother was in Charleston, and Jill was tending to the twins.

We gathered around a large conference table as a group of doctors entered the room in their white coats. Dr. Minton initiated the conversation, stating, "We have spent the last week evaluating Logan and monitoring his behavior, and we have reached a diagnosis with some new information we have gathered."

Everyone leaned in attentively as Dr. Minton continued, delivering shocking news. "Logan appears to be exhibiting classic symptoms being on the spectrum. We used to label it Autism but now we just say on the spectrum to cover it all. While many patients with this diagnosis are not typically violent, the substance abuse by his birth mother in utero exacerbates the symptoms and leads to violent behavior.

The weight of the revelation hit us, and we were filled with dismay. Dr. Minton continued, "After evaluating Logan's actions during his hospital stay and observing ongoing signs of disturbance, we are deeply concerned. His threats to harm himself and others cannot be dismissed. Just today, Logan expressed his intention to jump out of the window and hurt himself."

Ken's reaction revealed his shock, and Forrest inquired, "What is the treatment plan to address this?"

Dr. Minton responded, "Considering Logan's early onset, there is an elevated risk of him engaging in violence towards others. His aggressive behavior towards caregivers, inappropriate laughter, and unpredictable conduct can be attributed to his mental state. Additionally, the fetal drug exposure he experienced in the womb likely contributes to his lack of control and extreme irritability. While we cannot be certain due to Logan's age, we can conclude that he has a diagnosis of fetal drug exposure plus being on the spectrum. That's all the doctor would say.

I listened intently, sensing that the doctor had more to convey.

Dr. Minton continued, "The fetal drug damage severely impacts Logan's quality of life and necessitates ongoing treatment for the duration of his lifetime. As a family, you must consider the danger posed to Emma, given her young age. The risk of Emma being harmed by Logan due to his illness is significant. Violence within the home environment, regardless of the family member involved, can lead to chronic instability. However, Logan's chaotic behavior and the disharmony within your family could seriously impede Emma's development."

Forrest spoke up, seeking clarity. "What are you trying to say, Doctor?"

"Logan has been admitted to psychiatric wards multiple times, and as he grows older, his impairments and lack of control can worsen. I am deeply sorry for the immense suffering your family has endured. Considering the multiple risk factors, the team recommends placing Logan permanently in a residential treatment home," replied Dr. Minton.

Forrest exclaimed, "Are you serious?" Maureen let out a heavy sigh and began to cry. I struggled to catch my breath. Ken argued, "You mean right now? He's only seven years old!"

Dr. Minton allowed a moment of silence to let his words sink in. "It is not your fault that something is wrong with Logan's brain. We have adjusted his medication in the hopes of reducing some of his rage."

In all my years of practice, I have never seen a child as troubled as him," Dr. Minton explained.

I asked if I could see Logan.

Yes, you can see him. However, I need to prepare you for what happened last night. Logan had a tantrum that escalated, and he slammed his head into the floor, resulting in a gash that required sutures. Today has been a difficult day for him. He even lashed out at the therapy dog. When a patient becomes aggressive, we sometimes have to use restraints. This pushed him over the edge, and we had to sedate him, Dr. Minton informed me.

Silence enveloped the table. Dr. Minton continued, "Logan falls into a sad category: a sick child. I am deeply concerned for your safety, and I urge you to consider the options I have suggested. Finding an appropriate placement for him won't be easy, as there are very few treatment homes of this nature. I have already reached out to two residential facilities, but they have rejected him due to being at full capacity."

Dr. Posada interjected, "This ward is not designed for long-term care, and we must decide on Logan's discharge plan once his new medication regimen stabilizes."

I felt numb, as if all the air had been sucked out of the room, making it impossible to breathe. Ken's vacant stare revealed his struggle to comprehend the overwhelming information we had just received. Forrest held Maureen, comforting her as she silently wept on his shoulder.

CHAPTER 16

Against medical advice, Forrest insisted on bringing Logan home, determined to provide him with close care. He actively participated in Logan's treatment, becoming an integral part of his care team. My primary concern remained ensuring Emma's safety, and deep down, I feared Logan while recognizing the validity of the doctor's recommendations.

We decided to move Logan into Vera's apartment above the garage, while Vera relocated to the guest room in the main house. This arrangement allowed us to take shifts in caring for Logan. However, on the second night, Logan seized the moment and ran down the street, with Ken desperately chasing after him. It made me wonder how much more it would take for the Burnett's to give in. Perhaps they needed to experience some of the episodes that Vera and I had endured before consenting to place Logan in a residential treatment home.

We had raised and loved a child who had now become unsafe to be around. We had experienced immense anguish and faced numerous tragedies. Looking back, it's difficult to comprehend everything we went through. Logan existed in an entirely different reality. One with no remorse. He saw nonexistent shadows and exhibited irrationality. He would scream, "I want to hit, I want to hit," and lived in a state of unrest. He accused Emma of hiding his toys and taking his belongings, which led us to limit his contact with the main house and Emma, except for a special visit once a day.

Logan developed a strong aversion to the dark, necessitating him to turn on all the lights in the apartment during the night. He believed there were bugs that were not there.

Logan subjected me to long nights in the apartment. Fearful that he might escape and enter the main house, I hid the key to the deadbolt and locked myself in the second bedroom. One night, Logan appeared at my door and uttered, "I'm going to stab you." His destructive and unpredictable behavior instilled fear within our household. As a mother, I was tormented by his violent outbursts for which there seemed to be no explanation.

One of my journal entries reflects my state of mind during those challenging times:

"Frightened… behavior growing increasingly aggressive… we can't continue taking care of Logan. His behavior disturbs me.

His impulsiveness is concerning. His sleep patterns are disrupted again. Biting and screaming, he even threw hot coffee. I want to do what's best for Logan, but I feel like I can't handle this anymore."

The most painful part was witnessing Logan lash out at those who loved him and desperately wanted to help him. In the end, he drove everyone away. We all grew frustrated, and I yearned for a normal life for Emma.

Ken had reached his breaking point. The possibility of losing this child was immensely difficult for him to bear. He didn't want people to know. He didn't want to disappoint Forest. Logan's future appeared bleak, and his day to day was sad. Tearfully, Ken confided in his mother over the phone, saying, "It is so bad— why do I have to do this?"

Although I felt guilty for wanting Logan to be placed in a residential facility, given the torment he had brought upon our family, Emma's safety took precedence. Yet, Ken still allowed Logan to have supervised visits with her once a day. On one occasion, Logan became upset and climbed up on the outside of the staircase, unleashing his hatred upon Emma. A sense of terror enveloped Ken as he realized Logan was about to attack. Logan jumped on Emma's back while she fell to the floor, and he punched her mercilessly.

Once Ken managed to pull Logan off Emma, he noticed her bloody mouth from biting her lip during the fall. Emma was crying, so I carried her to the kitchen to assess her injuries. Applying pressure to her lip with a dishcloth to stop the bleeding, I cradled her head against my chest. Tenderly, I wrapped my arms around her and began rocking her while she sat on the counter, repeating, "Mommy's here. Mommy's here. It's okay, sweet girl."

I took Emma to her room and sat with her for a while. Then, I returned to the apartment and confronted Ken with a storm of fury. I said, enraged, "Logan has attacked Emma. It's time to place him in a facility." I glared at Ken, daring him to challenge me.

The situation in the house had escalated to a point where Logan's behavior became increasingly dangerous and uncontrollable. During one incident, Logan entered Ken's office, grabbed the cords from his laptop, and threatened to choke Ken to death. He proceeded to wrap the cords around his own neck, attempting self-harm, and then started hitting his own arm. In an effort to calm him down, Ken held Logan's head while I administered a pill to help him sleep, and he eventually drifted off while watching a movie.

It became abundantly clear to everyone involved that the level of care Logan required exceeded what our home could provide. Ken struggled deeply with accepting the fact that we had to place Logan in a facility. He was just worried about what Forrest would say. We mourned the loss of the dreams and hopes we had for Logan and grieved the loss of our child. It was an agonizing decision, as we were torn between our two children. Emma deserved a safe and normal life, while Logan's behavior posed a threat to everyone's well-being. Placing Logan away felt inherently wrong, but it seemed like the only choice we had.

Later that evening, Evelyn, Forrest, and Maureen came over, and Ken shared what had transpired and his decision to place Logan in a facility. Immediately, Evelyn took charge and started making calls. I overheard her assertively stating that a placement needed to be opened for Logan immediately, using her influence to ensure compliance. It was striking to witness how she skillfully handled difficult situations without becoming flustered, all while maintaining her southern charm.

Forrest's emotions began to overwhelm him, and with a cracked voice, he expressed his reservations about sending Logan away. Evelyn responded firmly, saying that their decision had moved beyond mere feelings and that Forrest needed to accept the reality of the situation. Evelyn said to Forest in secret, "This is your fault Forrest if you kept your hands off Emily we would not be in this situation." Forrest's heartbreak was evident, and Evelyn, in her unique way, told him to go away, recognizing the immense pain he was experiencing.

That night, Evelyn used every favor she had accumulated to secure Logan's immediate placement in the best residential facility home available. She went above and beyond by chartering a jet to transport him and a specialized psych nurse to his "new home" in Texas. I did not know why Logan's care was so important to Forrest and why Evelyn worked furiously to secure a home but one day soon this would all come to light.

The guilt I felt was consuming. Deep down, I knew that Ken blamed me for Logan's departure, feeling that I hadn't been a good enough mother to control him. Ken never managed to move past these sentiments, and the weight of that burden strained our relationship even more because Ken was so narcissistic. He had to blame someone and that someone was usually me. What I didn't know was the secret Ken was hiding for Forrest or the secret Forrest was hiding for Ken.

Ken's sensitivity and anger regarding Logan made him unwilling to discuss him with anyone. When questioned, he would simply mention that Logan had gone off to a boarding school, avoiding any mention of his illness. In contrast, I chose to be silent, seeing no reason to lie when the truth sufficed. However, I requested people to refrain from discussing Logan in front of Emma, as it was still too painful and raw for her. Additionally, I harbored guilt for feeling relieved that Logan was no longer part of our household, a feeling that brought deep shame and could only be shared with my counselor.

The therapist reassured me that experiencing relief after enduring a traumatic situation for seven years was normal. In fact, she likened her approach to treating me as she would a battered spouse. She identified my struggles with a version of Post-Traumatic Stress Disorder stemming from coping with Logan's behavior, which explained my heightened anxiety around crying children. She encouraged me to educate myself on Ken's narcissistic behavior as well.

It often felt like being in the midst of the Vietnam War with Logan, constantly on edge and finding it difficult to break those deeply ingrained habits. I shared with the counselor how I still found myself eating while standing, using the bathroom as quickly as possible, and rushing to wash my hands in the kitchen, as if I could still keep a watchful eye on Logan's actions, even though he was no longer there. Together, we humorously referred to it as being in "the Nam." Whenever I felt panic hearing children whine or cry, I would retreat into that mental space of being on high alert.

Through therapy, the counselor taught me techniques to manage the overwhelming emotions that stemmed from caring for an explosive child who had harmed me. I had become skilled at pretending and concealing my anxiety, as revealing it would only amplify Logan's reactions. However, now I needed to genuinely acknowledge and "sit with my feelings" instead of suppressing them.

Despite my love for Logan, despite not being my biological child, I couldn't escape the lingering guilt surrounding his placement. I had chosen Emma. Both children were adopted but I had bonded with Emma, not Logan. It led me to question if, deep down, I shared traits with Evelyn. She had always emphasized the importance of blood relations and the stronger obligations that exist within the family compared to those outside. Nevertheless, I remained fiercely protective of Emma, feeling compelled to spend the rest of my life compensating for the "lost years" that were never her fault. I prayed God would restore the years the locust had eaten.

Embracing the decision we made to place Logan away, I pondered how I could recover from such a loss. Apologies seemed futile. Ken and I had done what was necessary, and I no longer sought anyone's approval to find happiness. Instead, I resolved to maintain a positive outlook and trust that something new and better awaited our family. I had no desire to engage in unnecessary battles or convince others of my well-being—I simply focused on breathing in and out.

Having dedicated myself to raising Logan for seven years, it was now Emma's turn to receive my undivided attention once again. The counselor assured me that with time, the guilt associated with losing Logan would diminish, particularly as I redirected my focus toward Emma's well-being. She encouraged me to give Emma special attention. Emma, now 10, told me she wanted to find her birth parents. I replied that she could not even find her shoes. We laughed and hugged each other. I promised Emma we would look for her birth parents when she turned 18. Feeling she needed to be protected by whatever we found out being an adult seemed to be very important. I wondered if looking for Logan's birth parents made Emma start wondering about this. Emily never gave us any information and I wondered what she and her grandparents had hidden from us.

I used exercise as part of my healing process. It seemed to keep me sane I can still vividly recall my first day in that yoga room. Placing my mat on the floor, I lay down, allowing the warmth to seep into my muscles. With each deep breath, I let go of the day's burdens, feeling the tension melt away. Releasing negative emotions, they dropped off me, mingling with the drops of sweat falling to the ground.

Sometimes, letting go proves to be the best course of action, benefiting both my heart and state of mind. Finally, I caught a glimpse of a light at the end of this long, dark tunnel. Except without Logan I would have time for Ken. What did that even look like anymore?

CHAPTER 17

Our friend Mark had been a recovering alcoholic for a year and regularly attended men's AA meetings near his home with his wife Maggie. As part of his commitment to sobriety, Mark had taken on the role of sponsoring another man, Louis, who was in his mid-twenties. Together, they were working through the Twelve Step program as per AA practice.

One night, Maggie woke Mark up at 2:00 a.m., informing him that his phone was vibrating. When he answered the call, a voice on the other end identified themselves as the manager of O'Henry's Bar on Haywood Street. The manager explained that Louis was highly intoxicated and had mentioned Mark as someone who could come and pick him up.

Mark assured the manager that he would be there soon and asked for the bar's address. The manager described it as having a prominent sign on the door that read "Men's Night Out." Curious about the situation, Maggie asked Mark what was going on. He explained that he needed to go to O'Henry's Bar to get Louis because he was drunk. Maggie then inquired if the bar was a gay establishment, to which Mark confirmed. When she asked if he knew about Louis being gay, Mark replied that he did and emphasized that such information was confidential as he was Louis's sponsor.

After getting dressed, Mark drove to the bar with mixed feelings of disappointment in Louis's relapse and a commitment to support him through this challenging phase of his recovery. As he entered the bar, he noticed groups of men gathered in pairs or small groups. Scanning the room, he finally spotted Louis slumped over at the bar. Mark gently woke him and helped him to his feet, struggling to keep him steady as Louis's feet dragged along the floor.

While leaving the bar, Mark glanced over his shoulder and unexpectedly caught sight of Ken sitting in a booth with another man. The sight made Mark feel uneasy, prompting him to glance back again to confirm it was indeed Ken. Mark couldn't help but wonder why Ken was at a gay bar at two o'clock in the morning. Their eyes briefly met, and Ken quickly averted his gaze.

Mark drove Louis home and assisted him onto the couch, leaving a note saying he would pick him up for the upcoming AA meeting and help him retrieve his car afterward. It was nearly 3:30 a.m. when Mark finally crawled back into bed with Maggie, but the sight of Ken at the bar had unsettled him too much to sleep. Questions plagued his mind. What should he do about seeing Ken? Why was Ken there? Did Kate know about it? The next morning, Mark discussed the situation with Maggie, and they both agreed that he needed to talk to Ken.

While enroute to pick up Louis, Mark called Ken on the phone. When Ken answered, Mark straightforwardly asked, "Hey, what were you doing in that bar last night?" To Mark's surprise, Ken denied any involvement and stated that he was in Atlanta attending a conference. Mark's anger began to rise as he insisted that he saw Ken at O'Henry's. In response, Ken threatened to sue Mark for defamation of character, demanding that Mark not bring up the matter again before abruptly ending the call. Mark was furious and, in his rage, threw his cell phone out onto the highway.

Meanwhile, Vera, who was doing research on menopause for her mom using Ken's laptop in his home office, made a startling discovery. When she entered "menopause" into the search box, the drop-down history revealed terms such as "Men for Men." Vera immediately exclaimed, "Oh, Kate!" Witnessing Vera's reaction, Kate's face paled, and she knew they had stumbled upon something alarming. Determined to uncover the truth, Kate decided to hire a private investigator and instructed Vera to keep quiet about their findings regarding Ken.

Vera happened to know a local PI named John Jacobs, and Kate promptly contacted him for guidance. Kate explained her concerns, expressing her desire to determine if her husband was cheating or simply browsing gay porn. The PI requested a retainer, which Kate agreed to pay, and advised her to hire Eric, a computer expert, to examine Ken's laptop's hard drive for evidence of his online activities. Although Ken had been clearing the browsing history daily, the PI assured Kate that the information would still be stored on the hard drive. Kate arranged an appointment with the computer expert and promptly drove to his office, carrying the laptop to expedite the process.

Nervously awaiting the results, Kate observed as Eric delved into the laptop's hard drive. To her shock, he discovered a total of thirty visited gay websites, including explicit ones like barebacksex.com and babylonboys.com. Furthermore, Ken had conducted frequent searches related to "gay erotic stories" and "gay male massage." Understanding the gravity of the situation, Eric advised Kate to contact their cell phone provider for Ken's call records, suggesting that frequent numbers might offer further insights.

The scene overwhelmed me, shattering any illusions of a happy life. Seeking answers, I turned to Eric and asked about babylonboys.com. As he pulled up the website, my fury and fear intensified. It was a gay porn site featuring male models and live webcams for paid members seeking sexual content.

My mind raced with thoughts of the hedonistic life Ken was leading. Atlanta was a lie; the private investigator had discovered he was in Asheville all along, holed up in a hotel. Overwhelmed by everything I had learned, I dialed Ken's number without hesitation.

"Hello, how is your day going?" Ken's voice came through the line.

Struggling to maintain composure, I calmly inquired, "How's the conference in Atlanta?"

"It's the same old boring stuff as always," he replied.

That was it. I lost control. "I know you're lying and you're right here in Asheville!"

Ken grew agitated and denied it vehemently, blaming Mark for the misunderstanding. He claimed that Mark must have mistaken someone else for him at the bar. I informed him that I hadn't spoken to Mark or Maggie, and there was dead silence before Ken abruptly hung up on me.

Without wasting a moment, I immediately called Maggie, urging her to tell me everything. She explained the situation, how Mark wanted to confront Ken first, so she had promised to wait. She apologized for not informing me earlier, pleading for understanding in a difficult situation.

Upon entering the house, my fury was palpable to Vera. My hands trembled uncontrollably, rendering me unable to dial the phone, so I asked her to schedule a doctor's appointment for me. When she inquired why, I responded, "I want to get tested for STDs." Despite no longer needing her services, Vera still worked for us, as we had grown close like family after Logan's departure.

Once Vera finished making the call, I declared my intention to rid the house of my collection of Staffordshire Spaniel figurines. Every dog had to go. Some were valuable pieces from the 19th century, originating from England and Scotland. I adored the ones resembling King Charles Cavalier Spaniels. Grabbing each figurine set, I flung them into the fireplace, one after another. The rage inside me fueled my actions as I splintered them, loudly proclaiming the thousands of dollars they represented. "$1,000, $2,000… and more!" I cried out, relentlessly smashing them. The release was cathartic. "What a…!" I screamed, my voice filled with fury.

I couldn't bear the sight of those dogs anymore. It felt as though Ken had stabbed me and twisted the knife. "$7,000… this pair was from Monte Carlo." There was a thunderous crash, and Vera flinched with each set I threw into the fireplace. Ceramic shards scattered, and I yearned to blow up the house, eradicating everything within.

Vera hesitantly questioned if I truly wanted to continue destroying them, reminding me of Ken's anger when Logan had broken one last year. "Ken will erupt when he realizes I've obliterated $15,000 worth of collectibles."

"He deserves some payback for his horrible actions," Vera agreed, acknowledging the need for retribution.

"He was with me when we bought each and every one of these sets," I explained. "We were supposed to showcase our collection next month at the Staffordshire Figurine Collectors meeting that Veranda was hosting. Now that I know he was cheating, I want to purge the house of every last figurine."

As Vera struggled to contain the heavy bag of shattered pieces, she went to get another one. My determination was unwavering— I needed to remove every dog from the house and dispose of them in the garage's garbage toter. "I can't bear to look at them anymore. How dare he do this to me!"

"Every vacation, every trip, Ken and I shopped for Staffordshire dogs," I confessed, fueled by adrenaline and outrage. "I was building a collection, and Ken was collecting men. These figurines were his trophies from his escapades with every lover he had."

"It's a shame Logan isn't here; he would have relished smashing these," Vera chimed in, reminiscing about happier times.

Overwhelmed by a mix of grief and betrayal, I couldn't bear to remain in the house, surrounded by painful reminders. It was a constant struggle—mourning the loss of Logan and grappling with the mutilated trust in Ken. Emma and I desperately needed an escape, a respite from the turmoil that threatened to consume us. With a heavy heart, I asked Vera to help me pack a bag for Emma as we planned to leave town immediately. I simply had to get us out of that suffocating environment.

Fuelled by a seething anger, I loaded the bags into the car and embarked on a journey with Emma by my side. Our destination: Atlanta. Seeking solace and refuge, we sought shelter at the Ritz Carlton, an oasis where we could momentarily forget our troubles. While Emma had been to the Ritz before, this particular visit held a profound significance for me. As we approached the grand entrance, the familiar valet greeted us with a warm smile, saying, "Welcome back," as if we were returning to a place we belonged.

Walking through the opulent lobby, I couldn't help but share my personal belief with Emma—that the Ritz was akin to a heavenly retreat, where even God would choose to spend a day off from His celestial duties. Her face lit up with a smile as she took in the breathtaking floral arrangements and the shimmering brilliance of the chandeliers above. Making our way to the reception, I requested a generously sized suite, charging it to my trusted American Express card. At that moment, I declared to Emma that she had stepped foot into the Motherland, a sanctuary of luxury and comfort amidst our tumultuous lives.

As we settled onto the plushness of the hotel bed, Emma's curiosity about the Ritz sparked a conversation. I eagerly shared my admiration for their impeccable service, emphasizing the allure of the room's elegant dark wood floors. With a sense of contentment, Emma soaked in the atmosphere, while we indulged in room service and perused the enticing array of in- room movies. Eventually, Emma's choice fell upon a heartwarming tale about penguins. Our luggage arrived promptly, and the attentive baggage attendant took a moment to inform Emma that the sheets boasted a remarkable 1000 thread count. Her fingers glided gently over the luxurious fabric, marveling at its softness. The attendant proudly attributed the extraordinary comfort to the exceptionally high thread count.

Meanwhile, back in Atlanta, the tenacious private investigator, John, remained dedicated to his surveillance of Ken. Following Ken's movements from the hotel, John meticulously tracked his entrance into an exclusive men's club after a brief stroll down the street. Intrigued by what lay beyond those doors, John decided to gain access by registering as a member and paying the requisite fee. What he discovered within the club's walls was a world of exposed bodies, towels, and explicit encounters. Rooms lined the hallways, each offering various amenities and opportunities for anonymous sexual liaisons. Among the sea of men, John couldn't help but notice one individual wearing a wedding ring—a stark reminder of the complexity of human desires. Continuing his investigation, John found Ken stationed in a social lounge, waiting with a sense of anticipation. Although the environment made

John uncomfortable, he remained in the lounge for a while longer, observing the dynamics at play before finally making his exit. Ken eventually showered, engaged in conversation with other men by the poolside, and eventually made his way back to the hotel.

In the solitude of the Ritz's bathroom, I sought a moment of privacy. Turning on the shower to muffle the sound of my voice, I perched on the edge of the luxurious marble tub, enveloped in the soft embrace of the plush white robe against my skin. Emma was peacefully asleep, and the closed bathroom door provided a semblance of seclusion. Gazing at my reflection in the polished white marble floor, I dialed the phone, poised to receive the crucial information I sought.

"Hello, Mrs. Burnett," John's voice came through the phone. "Please, call me Kate. What did Ken do today?" I asked anxiously. "Where did he go?"

"You may want to sit down, Kate…" John's words hung heavy in the air, causing my breath to catch. Overwhelmed with anticipation and dread, I dialed another number, desperately seeking support and solace. "The report I just received from the private investigator about Ken… it's shocking. I had no idea about the extent of his involvement in the gay lifestyle. He's fully immersed."

The sound of my sister's voice on the other end of the line weakened my resolve. Collapsing onto the cold marble floor, I gave in to the overwhelming pain and sobbed. I was utterly broken. Just when I thought I couldn't bear any more heartache after losing my precious little boy, Ken had inflicted another betrayal upon me. Through tears and gasps, I poured out my heart to Jill, sharing the devastating details of what I had just discovered. Grateful for the running shower and the locked bathroom door, I hid my anguish, knowing that Emma must never see me in such a vulnerable state. For Emma's sake, I had to find strength and the anger of it all gave me the strength to keep it together. From total devastation you start over, you find a way.

"We're on our way to the Ritz and will be there in a few hours," Jill assured me. "Hold yourself together for Emma." Then, I heard her say, "Momma, you and I are going to Atlanta to be with Kate and Emma. Kate just found out that Ken is gay and has been cheating on her with men. So, we're driving down to the Ritz. Emma will stay with you, and you can keep her entertained while I help Kate navigate through this."

My mother buried her face in her hands, overcome with a mixture of grief and disbelief. "First Logan, and now this?" she thought, her tears mingling with the weight of the sorrow that had already burdened her heart.

CHAPTER 18

Our mom Mimi, and Emma stayed in one room at the Ritz so Jill and I could have some privacy in another room for lengthy discussions about our next steps. The first thing on my agenda was to drive by the men-only clubs in Atlanta. There were four main clubs, some of which were converted warehouses while others were bathhouses. The particular club where Ken had been followed by the PI had a nondescript front door, tinted to conceal the interior, with a sign that boldly proclaimed it as a "Men's Only Private Club." I couldn't fathom that this was where Ken spent his time when he was supposed to be working. Numbness enveloped me, but Jill urged me to stop pretending that everything was okay.

Meanwhile, John, the private investigator I had hired, continued to tail Ken and document his encounters. When he called me with his latest findings, I was utterly incredulous.

Ken had taken a trip to Fantasy Festival in Ft. Lauderdale with David Talent, a single man and long-time friend who lived in our neighborhood. I had always suspected that David might be gay.

To my astonishment, the PI discovered that David was Ken's steady boyfriend, yet Ken continued to engage in casual sexual encounters with other men. He was cheating on both his boyfriend and me. He was a true narcissist, deriving pleasure from the act of cheating and the thrill of secrecy. He reveled in the danger of being caught, firmly believing that he would never face exposure. He engaged in risky behavior solely for the adrenaline supply it provided.

Shockingly, Ken took me out to lunch at the club one day, only to rendezvous with our waiter for a sexual encounter later that afternoon.

It was excruciating to hear these revelations about my husband. Initially, shame washed over me, swiftly followed by a seething fury. I couldn't comprehend that Ken was capable of such actions. John, empathetic to my plight, offered his apologies, but I expressed gratitude for his efforts in uncovering the truth so that I could confront it head-on.

When Ken returned home two days later, he acted as if nothing were amiss. He hastily greeted Emma with a kiss and retreated to the shower. Still reeling from John's reports, I was repulsed by Ken's presence yet desperate for confirmation from his "boyfriend." Without hesitation, I seized his cell phone and dialed David Talent's number. When David answered, I abruptly hung up, my heart pounding. Then, summoning all my courage, I redialed the number. The phone rang, and David's voice came through, saying, "Ken, are you there?" Breathless, I disconnected the call once again.

Incensed, yet longing to confront Ken with undeniable proof, I entered the master bathroom, clutching his phone tightly. "How long have you been having an affair with David Talent?" I demanded, my voice trembling with a mix of anger and pain. Without missing a beat, Ken replied, "Why don't you just go ahead and announce my 'big secret' to everyone?" Caught off guard by his response, I could only place his phone on the bathroom counter and leave the room in a daze.

In the kitchen, my mind raced with conflicting emotions as Ken entered and attempted to downplay the situation. "I have no idea what you're talking about. I suppose from now on, you'll assume I'm sleeping with every man I come into contact with. David is just a friend from high school, nothing more. You really need to calm down, or I'll tell everyone you had affairs throughout our entire marriage."

"You lied to me! Our marriage vows have been shattered! You cheated and lied! It doesn't matter you've been living a secret life," I cried, my voice filled with anguish.

"I expected you to stop dating when we got married. I'm furious... you've been unfaithful throughout our entire marriage. I know because I've checked the hard drives of every computer we've owned, even the old desktop, dating back to our early years together. I know everything," I declared, my voice filled with a mixture of hurt and anger.

Ken's response was callous. "Look, you were just on the rebound from losing the love of your life, and I was the perfect Band-Aid for your situation. It's not like I was your soul mate or anything," he retorted dismissively.

"You don't deserve me!" I sobbed, my heart breaking. "I loved you as my husband and the father of our children. You merely tolerated me to maintain the facade of a heterosexual relationship, making me doubt myself as a woman. I did everything in my power to make myself attractive to you, but you deceived yourself more than you deceived me. Living a lie is no way to exist. How do you sleep at night, lying in bed beside me while cheating on me throughout our entire marriage? I feel so humiliated!"

When I mustered the courage to inform Ken that I wanted a divorce, he erupted in a rage, refusing to accept it. "We are staying married! We will not get a divorce!" he bellowed, before issuing a chilling threat. "I will take Emma away from you and expose you as a pill addict or an alcoholic. I'll prove that you're an unfit mother, and my family will use their influence to ensure it sticks."

He exuded threatening confidence, convinced he would emerge victorious.

As Ken's true nature and manipulative tendencies became apparent, a chilling fear gripped me. It became clear that he cared more about winning and maintaining his image than about the well-being of Emma and me. Despite my fear, I couldn't let him off the hook this time. I stood my ground and asserted that Emma was the most important person in my life, and I only wanted what was best for her. I acknowledged that he would always be her father, but I refused to let him control our lives any longer.

I confronted Ken with the knowledge I had gathered about his secret encounters, including his involvement with gay men through dating services and dating apps. I revealed that I had hired a private investigator who had evidence of his actions. Furthermore, I confronted him about Aunt Evie's attempts to subject him to reparative therapy and conversion therapy, realizing that these efforts had only reinforced his behavior. I explained that he had become trapped in a pattern that couldn't be easily broken, and it saddened me to acknowledge that the man I thought I knew was nothing but a facade. His narcissistic tendencies bordered on emotional abuse.

Ken's treatment of me as his property fueled my anger. I had been a faithful and devoted wife for over a decade. Who admits to having lovers throughout their entire marriage? As memories resurfaced, things began to make sense. I recalled our trip to France, where Ken had arranged for massages with both male and female therapists. He had chosen a male therapist despite my indifference, later leaving me alone for dinner while he said he went out shopping. He returned empty-handed. Jill had questioned his actions, sensing that something was amiss. We later agreed he went out with the massage therapist.

Another memory surfaced, a conversation in which Ken had given a feeble excuse for our lack of intimacy, claiming that seeing Emma being born had diminished his interest in sex. I had been surprised, as I believed men desired beautiful women constantly. Ken never touched me.

Finally, I mustered the courage to ask Ken if he had ever loved me. His response was silence. When I pressed further, asking how he felt about me, he coldly replied, "Indifferent."

"Why did you marry me?" I inquired desperately. Ken's answer struck me to the core. "You still had faith in people. You were so naive, believing that people were essentially good. You were heartbroken and vulnerable. It was easy to sweep you off your feet. You fell for the whole act, hook, line, and sinker. You were conned. Deal with it, Kate. Grow up! It happened so easily… like something out of a fairy tale. But it happened. Get over it. You're not leaving me, and I won't admit to anyone that I'm gay. I'll never give you a divorce, and I'll never leave this house. You'll stay here for Emma and pretend that nothing has changed. Got it!" he yelled as he pointed his finger in my face.

Ken threw a bar stool across the room.

But I couldn't accept any of that. I shook my head defiantly. Ken taunted me, asking, "What are you going to do about it? You really don't know, do you?" Ken grew dark. He was disclosing a juicy secret because he was angry.

What? I said, sounding afraid.

"Logan is my half-brother. He was Forrest and Emily's son. We paid off her family and sent her away.

My heart raced as I stumbled to sit down. The long-buried Burnett secrets hidden deep with the family's history were now out. Logan was the bastard son of Forrest and Ken was gay. My mind was gripped by a sense of dread and as the pieces slowly fell into place, my world shattered around me. The revelation he uncovered was beyond my worst nightmare- a twisted web of deception, betrayal, and unspeakable horrors that had been concealed for years. The weight of this newfound knowledge bore down on me leaving me breathless and shaken. I was confronted with the haunting truth that had forever altered my perception of family and identity. Ken told me with such ease like it was no big deal and he was enjoying it.

With pain and determination in my voice, I whispered, "Look at the deception that constantly surrounds me! You will pay for all the evil you've done to me. I am finished with your lies and your control. Your heart is empty. Your family is so dysfunctional and sick."

Mockingly, Ken suggested that I return to the trailer he had found me in and embrace the supposed "white trash" I supposedly was. His cruel words pierced through me, and I couldn't believe the lengths he would go to hurt me. "I married you and the life you promised me, Ken, but I also expected you to love me," I lamented.

Ken callously admitted that he was incapable of loving me and I was just a pawn. That was the moment I resolved not to stay married to him any longer. I began to protect my heart from further pain and told him, "If you want to have relationships with other men, then go ahead. Just let me go. Leave me out of it. I want away from you and your family."

Ken's revelation about his family's knowledge of him being gay and their intention to use me as a cover for their image made me realize I was used by more than one person. The pain overwhelmed me, and I silently let tears stream down my face, burying my emotions deep within, just as I had done with Logan.

But Ken's demeaning words continued to pour out. He called me stupid and revealed that his family had orchestrated our marriage, knowing he was gay. He admitted that he had used me to maintain appearances and fulfill his desire for children. According to him, I was to accept this reality and remain silent, as divorce was out of the question. He warned me of the fierce battle I would face if I dared to challenge him, with his family siding against me to take Emma away. He continued to threaten me, enjoying seeing me fear him. He said his father would take me down if I revealed anything I found out. I believed him.

Anger boiled within me, old resentments and repressed rage resurfacing. I couldn't contain it any longer. Looking Ken directly in the eyes, with a newfound determination, I unleashed my pent- up fury. I told him I wanted a divorce, accusing him of treating me like a maid, burdening me with childcare, household chores, a job, and entertaining guests. I emphasized my loyalty, faithfulness, and dedication as a wife, and condemned his disrespectful treatment. The thought of potential diseases he could have exposed me to filled me with disgust.

Ken callously replied, "No, they always used a condom." His response only fueled the fight. I sarcastically remarked, "Oh, you were the one receiving. That's just perfect."

The realization that Ken had engaged in affairs, one-night stands, and casual sex during our marriage hit me hard. It shattered the illusion of him being my friend or husband. I confronted him, expressing my disbelief and pain, while he coldly asserted that he felt sorry for me. He never cared for me. This family never cared for me.

"How long did you go without a lover during our marriage?" I asked, my voice filled with bitterness.

"Three months," Ken replied matter-of-factly.

I reminded him of the stark contrast between his treatment of me behind closed doors and in public. He had treated me like a possession in private while parading me as royalty in front of others. That was why I had always wanted to entertain guests, seeking validation and a semblance of happiness. Now, I had a legitimate reason to divorce him and escape this suffocating existence. Ken hadn't wanted a wife; he had wanted an incubator, a nanny, a maid, a baby sitter, and an arm piece. I questioned why he hadn't simply hired a surrogate.

"Things were different when we got married," Ken defended himself. "You couldn't just be gay and out. I was gay before it was acceptable and my father would not be accepting it."

My mind spun, memories flooding back as pieces fell into place. I recalled how Ken never looked at other women, never exhibited jealousy when men flirted with me, and always prioritized his appearance. I remembered stumbling upon gay porn on the computer screen, which he dismissed as a pop-up but reacted angrily when caught. He would rush to take a shower as soon as he came home, never showing any physical affection towards me.

Everything became clear, and I felt like a fool for not realizing the truth earlier. Years of effort I had put into trying to please him, from lingerie to tan lines, perfume to new hairstyles, all the attempts to gain his attention. I now realized that there was nothing I could have done to entice him. He didn't want me but he was determined to make me stay just because he thought he could.

The desire for freedom overwhelmed me. I wanted to escape this absurd prison that Ken had ensnared me in. But I worried about Emma, caught in the middle of our fight especially after losing her adopted brother. Who was actually not her brother at all? Lies have a unique way of compounding over time, weaving intricate webs of deceit that grow more tangled and complex with each falsehood. With each layer of deception, the weight of the lies intensifies, placing immense pressure on the liar to maintain consistency and avoid exposure. Eventually, the lies became a burden, straining relationships, eroding trust, and distorting reality. The compounded lies create a fragile facade that can crumble with the slightest disturbance, revealing the devastating consequences of a tangled web built upon deceit.

Ken's vindictiveness and thirst for retaliation loomed over me, and I couldn't predict what he would do next. Yet, I had reached a point where I no longer cared. He had pushed me too far. My emotional and mental limits were surpassed leading to the breaking point. My goal now was to get out and restore balance to my life. But I had to be careful even if I was pissed because he was mean.

During a shopping trip, I bought a sarcastic doormat. Recognizing the subtle innuendo, I couldn't resist the opportunity to provoke Ken and make him mad. I purchased the doormat and placed it by the garage door, knowing it would serve as a reminder of his secrets and lies.

CHAPTER 19

As the days and weeks passed, my determination to pursue the divorce grew stronger, but I couldn't shake the heartbreak that consumed me. I realized that I had been so enamored by the Burnett family's facade and their acceptance of me that I had been blind to the truth. Looking back, I could now see many signs that should have raised red flags about Ken's behavior.

One such sign was his refusal to wear his wedding ring to the pool or the beach, claiming he didn't want a tan line. I now felt foolish for not realizing that he used it as an opportunity to cheat without leaving any visible indication of his marriage. I had been completely blind to his infidelity because I trusted him wholeheartedly. But now, the truth had come crashing down, contaminating our marriage and poisoning it completely.

When Ken received notice of my divorce filing, he was furious.

That night, he confronted me, asking if there was something I needed to tell him. He mentioned receiving a receipt for a lawyer's retainer in the mail and demanded that I refund the money immediately, emphasizing his disdain for surprises.

"What did you expect me to do, Ken? Once I found out, I had to take action. I have always done everything you asked of me and been a faithful wife. What hurts the most is that I have given my all through the good and the bad, holding our relationship together like glue. But you kept pulling away, stopped fighting for me, and only fought with me. You don't put in any effort anymore. We can't buy happiness; we are either happy or not. It's evident that you are not happy in this marriage and never will be," I explained, my voice filled with pain.

Ken cynically responded, acknowledging that I had caught him but asserting that I would never walk away from the money, showing no concern for the emotional toll it had taken on me. He demanded I get the money back. With a haughty laugh, he left the room, truly believing that I would never leave him.

Later that evening, as I kissed Emma goodnight, she asked me why her parents were getting a divorce and if it was because he loved someone else. I reassured her that we both loved her very much, and this was not her fault or mine. I promised to explain everything when she was older. Thankfully, she didn't press for more details, and I stayed with her until she fell asleep.

Feeling overwhelmed, I called my mom in Charleston, confessing my guilt and humiliation for not seeing through Ken's deception. My mom shared that she, too, had been conned by him and urged me not to blame myself. The conversation and learning that he had fooled my mom as well helped alleviate some of the pain.

In a desperate attempt to hurt me further, Ken began spreading rumors that I had been unfaithful, using it as the supposed reason for our failing marriage. He claimed I had slept with our nanny, Vera, and my boss at work.

When I discovered the lies Ken was spreading, anger surged through me, clouding my vision. I immediately called him to confront him. I couldn't believe his audacity. "How dare you say that I had affairs? While you were busy pursuing others, I was consumed with taking care of Logan. If I must, I will take a polygraph test to prove my faithfulness throughout our entire marriage," I declared, my voice filled with righteous anger. But once again, he hung up on me.

Next, I reached out to Vera, informing her about Ken's lies. I wanted her to be aware of what he was spreading. I reassured her, saying, "No offense, but I am not attracted to tall women." Vera laughed, understanding the situation, and responded, "None taken. I would never do you, but I know you want my fabulous braids." We shared a laugh.

It felt good to have someone on my side, someone who could laugh with me amidst the chaos. Vera was more than a confidant; she was a friend.

Jill and Travis, who had been supporting me throughout this ordeal, arranged for me to take a polygraph exam with a certified licensed examiner. On the day of the appointment, I arrived at the office and was greeted by Mr. McCallister, a professional-looking man with white hair. He led me into the testing room, where he explained the process and the questions he would ask. Nervously, I signed the consent forms.

With the video camera recording our session, Mr. McCallister placed leads on various parts of my body. He explained that he would measure my breathing, pulse, and galvanic skin responses while asking the questions. And so, the polygraph examination began.

Mr. McCallister asked the following questions, and I answered "No" to each one:

- Since your marriage to Ken Burnett, have you had sexual relations with anyone else?
- Did you ever have sex with a boss or co-worker?
- Did you ever have sexual relations with Vera, your nanny?

I awaited the results, hoping that this test would help put an end to Ken's malicious lies.

After Mr. McCallister confirmed the truthfulness of my polygraph test results, I felt a renewed sense of empowerment. Finally, I had concrete evidence that validated my feelings and disproved Ken's lies. With a smile on my face, I made copies of the eight-page report, including Mr. McCallister's impressive credentials, and decided to send them to certain individuals.

The recipients were Aunt Evie, Forrest, and Maureen, and some of Ken's family members. Another copy went to Robert, Ken's brother, who surprised me by admitting that he knew Ken was lying about all the things I was accused of. It was a relief to have someone from his family acknowledge the truth.

Aunt Evelyn, however, rejected the letter by marking "Return to Sender" on the envelope. Seeing it back in my mailbox, I knew she had read every word, likely through Forrest's copy, and refused the letter as a way to spite me. They all knew about Ken's true sexual preferences but wanted to keep it a secret.

A week or two later, as I sat on the front porch reading, Lee Yung, a young gay man who managed the grocery store, noticed me and stopped his car. Lee, around thirty years old and in graduate school, offered me words of comfort and reassurance. He said it wasn't my fault and that I had done nothing wrong. Surprisingly, Lee mentioned that he knew Ken was gay from the moment he met us, based on Ken's eye contact and mannerisms.

Lee went on to explain how things had changed in terms of relationships and sexual dynamics. He shared stories of open marriages and group sex, emphasizing that it had become more common and accepted in some circles. As he spoke, I realized how sheltered I had been, especially due to my focus on caring for Logan over the past seven years. It was eye-opening to hear about these aspects of sexuality that I had been unaware of.

Curiously, I asked Lee about the prevalence of threesomes, to which he responded with a look of pity. It dawned on me that I was sexually inexperienced and naive, and Ken had preferred it that way. Throughout our marriage, he had never been willing to explore sexual experimentation with me, leaving me feeling oblivious to the broader spectrum of sexual experiences. These were concepts that seemed foreign and overwhelming.

My thoughts shifted to the challenges of dating in a world where pornography was easily accessible, and I couldn't help but wonder how I would fit into this new sexual landscape. I shared my college experience of only seeing couples and not even knowing what a "ménage à trois" was. Ken's reluctance to having sex before marriage was due to strong morals he convinced me; not realizing his disinterest in women.

Lee laughed and reassured me, reemphasizing that I had done nothing wrong and that I was a beautiful woman. He also mentioned the high population of gay men in the neighborhood, further deepening my sense of being deceived.

After my conversation with Lee, I grew concerned about Emma's future experiences in the dating world. I wondered what she would face and how society's evolving attitudes toward sex would impact her. It was a realization that left me chuckling at the irony of the intense gossip within the church community, completely oblivious to the truth about Ken.

Later that week, the Burnett family called a meeting to address the "situation." Although I wasn't involved, Robert, surprisingly, shared all the details with me. He expressed sympathy for what I was going through and wondered how I would handle everything. He also admitted to thoroughly enjoying watching his brother face the consequences of his actions.

After Robert filled me in on the family meeting, he eagerly recounted the heated confrontation between Aunt Evelyn and Ken. Aunt Evie wasted no time in confronting Ken about his sexuality, adamant that she would drag him out of the closet, even if she had to physically do it herself. Robert couldn't resist injecting some humor, jokingly suggesting that it would make Ken a "drag queen." However, Aunt Evie didn't find it amusing and promptly silenced him, ordering him to shut up. Evelyn informed Forrest to back off Ken and let him come out. Forrest agreed to keep the focus off him. Robert said they just wanted to make sure I would not talk about family secrets.

Being a congressional candidate, Aunt Evelyn saw Ken's coming out as a golden opportunity to champion gay rights in her campaign. She believed the timing was perfect to bring this issue to the forefront and incorporate it into her political platform. Blaming Ken for his carelessness in frequenting a gay bar in Asheville, Aunt Evie asserted that they could no longer contain the truth. Robert couldn't help but add a sardonic remark, pointing out that Aunt Evie was supposed to be preoccupied with her own affairs in Atlanta, not meddling locally.

Maureen, Ken's mother, instinctively rushed to his defense, expressing concern about how his coming out would impact Emma. However, Aunt Evie shot her a withering look, dismissing her worries with a cutting remark. In her view, it was too late to salvage the situation, as Ken's lack of caution had exposed the truth. Determined, Aunt Evelyn declared that they would proceed with breaking the story, already enlisting a team to handle the matter.

The discussion then turned to me, as Forrest inquired about my fate in light of these revelations. Aunt Evie nonchalantly brushed me aside, deeming me expendable and sharing that my office had been packed up, the locks changed, and security instructed me not to grant me access. Adding salt to the wound, she revealed that my work cell had been disconnected, severing my ties to the company.

Robert couldn't resist fueling the tension further, recounting Ken's musical preferences during high school. Maureen scolded Robert for his remarks, and Aunt Evie swiftly silenced him, issuing a threatening warning that left no room for further comments.

Just as the tension reached its peak, Aunt Evelyn's cell phone rang, prompting her to silence the whole family as she answered the call. With a notepad in hand, she diligently jotted down notes, repeating the instructions out loud:

- "Join PFLAG."
- "Show support at Pride functions."
- "March in Washington in June."
- "Divorce Kate discreetly, throwing unwavering support behind same-sex marriage and gay rights."
- "Secure joint custody of Emma, emphasizing Ken's devotion as a father."

After the call concluded, Aunt Evelyn shared her strategy: she intended to leverage Ken as the face of her campaign, gay rights, and same-sex marriage. To achieve this, she planned to orchestrate Ken's life to extract maximum benefits for her political aspirations. Ken and David would openly live together, standing by Aunt Evelyn's side as they participated in a gay march in Washington DC that June. They would spin the narrative of the divorce, Ken's revelation of being gay, and his relationship with David to their advantage, capitalizing on every aspect for the sake of the campaign.

Ken had always relied on his wealth to compensate for his deep- rooted self-esteem issues stemming from leading a secret life. Now, he was forced to face his true self and live openly as a gay man. Only time would tell if Ken possessed the strength and resilience to navigate this uncharted territory within the confines of Asheville society. As societal attitudes shifted and evolved, even the traditionally conservative Burnett family found themselves in the midst of transformative change.

CHAPTER 20

As Ken's relentless attacks on my character took a toll on me, a glimmer of excitement emerged when Maggie called and suggested going out to dinner. Eager to escape the turmoil, we met at a restaurant and each ordered a glass of wine, ready to unload and discuss everything that was transpiring. When Maggie shared the absurdity of seeing Ken and David parading through the neighborhood on new Vespa scooters, I couldn't help but shake my head in disbelief. The hilarity of her comment almost made me spit wine across the table as we both burst into laughter.

"How could I have been so oblivious?" I wondered aloud.

"Honey, Ken had us all fooled, although his obsession with Burberry Plaid should have been a dead giveaway," Maggie replied.

"Yes, you're right. That should have raised a red flag," I acknowledged, realizing in hindsight that there were countless signs I had missed. Living with Ken had always been a challenge, with everything revolving around him.

"You're not kidding!" I concurred. "He's spending a fortune dragging me to court, deliberately making my life a living hell. Without fail, right before we enter the courtroom, his lawyer huddles with mine and proposes a deal. But it still costs me $3,000 every time my attorney prepares to face the judge." Maggie's expression turned sour. "That's terrible, Kate."

"It's all part of Ken's plan," I sighed. "He knows I can't afford the legal fees, and I'm drowning in debt just trying to keep up. My mom gave me $10,000 to assist with the attorney. It was not a drop in the bucket. I can't keep asking her for help. She's living on a fixed income now."

Maggie questioned the cruelty of Ken's actions, considering he was the one who had engaged in secret affairs. "Why is he so ugly?" she wondered.

"Ken is an emotionally immature man-child with a penchant for excessive spending," I replied sarcastically. "He thrives on pushing me to the brink, wanting me to suffer the consequences of exposing his true self. Financially crippling me is just one of his many tactics to hurt me."

Maggie attempted to lighten the mood, noting, "Consider yourself lucky. You deserve better than a narcissistic gay man." I couldn't help but snicker, responding that the only action our bedroom saw was when I hit the snooze button.

The laughter nourished my soul as I relaxed in the cozy mahogany booth, savoring the moment with my dear friend. However, amidst the joy, the weight of my struggles loomed large in my thoughts. Suddenly, I remembered another incident. While shopping with my friend Belinda, she had shown me a foundation in a tube with a brush attached to it. She highly recommended it for its excellent coverage, and I decided to purchase one. Yet, when the sales clerk attempted to process my credit card, it was embarrassingly declined. Belinda, understanding the situation, stepped in and graciously bought it for me.

Maggie couldn't believe it and asked what had happened. I explained that Ken had canceled all my credit cards, suspended my cell service, and stopped paying for our health insurance. "Travis, Jill's husband, warned me that just when I thought things couldn't get any worse, they would," I recounted. "He advised me to be cautious and prepared, and sadly, he was right."

"I'm so sorry, honey," Maggie consoled me, her unwavering support always by my side.

Then, the conversation shifted to the living situation between Ken and me. "I hate it," I confided. "Ken spends fifteen nights a month with Emma, and I have her for the remaining fifteen. The rest of the time, I bounce between staying with family while Ken stays with David. It's incredibly stressful, constantly moving in and out. But that's the arrangement the lawyers worked out to avoid uprooting Emma from her familiar surroundings."

"Oh, and here's another gem," I added. "When Ken leaves, he takes half of my shoes with him." Maggie couldn't believe her ears. I explained that Ken intentionally ensured I wouldn't have a matching pair of shoes, so I resorted to packing my clothes and keeping suitcases in my car.

"That's insane, Kate. You can't continue living like this," Maggie asserted.

Jo Ann and Belinda finally joined us. As they settled in and ordered their own drinks they insisted on a recap of the conversation Maggie and I had been having. After bringing them up to speed, Jo Ann interjected, "Kate, you have to move out. This is beyond ridiculous." I informed them that Ken had adamantly refused to leave the house and had sworn never to pay any alimony or child support. The girls stared at me, incredulous. Jo Ann voiced their collective thoughts, "What kind of father refuses to support his own daughter?" Belinda chimed in, "Haven't you been through enough already, losing Logan and then discovering Ken's infidelity."

Jo Ann mentioned a house for rent near her, suggesting that it might be a good idea for me to move out. After discussing it with my friends, I realized they were right. Belinda expressed her opinion, saying, "Ken will never leave that house, and you can't keep living like this. One of you has to move." Maggie agreed, adding, "Since Ken refuses to sell the house, you should leave."

I responded, "I think you're right. My sister must be tired of me staying with her for fifteen days each month. Besides, I need my own space where I can relax."

Jo Anne shared some interesting information, saying, "Ken lives at his lover's house on the fifteen days he is not with Emma. The drinks were flowing, and my friends were getting bolder with their advice.

Belinda continued, "Nobody understands how devastating and life-destroying this has been for you, Kate. You need to move out, move on, and start some dating." Maggie joined in, saying, "That's right. Your corpse of a marriage has long been cold."

I replied, "Yes, Ken and David have been together a lot longer than people think. Despite their promiscuity, they function like a couple. Now that Evelyn is running for North Carolina Congress, she is advocating for gay rights and is supporting Ken's gay lifestyle. She is also using mental illness awareness as a platform, and the Center she is building is almost completed."

Jo Ann inquired, "Oh, how is Logan doing?"

"I really don't know," I admitted. "The Burnett's won't give me an update. The last I heard, he was in a residential treatment home in Texas. It was a ranch for boys. Emma mentioned reading an email to Ken, stating that Logan doesn't have the ability to miss us. No remorse. Logan is emotionally different. He seems happy when visually stimulated outside but never asks about us. Logan doesn't have the ability to bond to anyone." I knew not to share anymore and didn't want to talk about Logan. The family secret needed to stay buried to protect me and Emma.

"Kate, I am so sorry," Jo Anne sympathized.

Feeling a mix of emotions, I responded, "I'm dealing with the guilt of not raising Logan and the guilt of feeling relieved at not having to."

"You did the best you could, Kate," Maggie comforted, putting her arm around me. "No one could handle him. Logan is where he needs to be."

Belinda chimed in, "Girls, let's get Kate started on dating!" We really needed to cut Belinda off. Jo Anne enthusiastically joined in, saying, "Kate gets a do-over! Count me in." Belinda added, "Kate, you need to get a new job and move out. I can get you a job as a loan officer at the bank where I work!"

I never thought my motto would be "eat, drink, and remarry." I wasn't sure where life was taking me. But if I were honest, I would admit I was lonely. Emma was at the age where she only wanted to be with her friends and all of my friends were married. I had felt this way for a long time because I was alone for the decade I was married to Ken. He never loved me so we were never close.

He was mean so I never let him in.

Not long after that dinner with my friends, I signed the lease for a rental house a few streets away from Ken. He wasn't pleased that I was moving out and threw a tantrum when I asked about dividing the furniture. Eventually, he reluctantly agreed to go through the house and mark with sticky notes anything he wanted to keep. I was just relieved to be out of that house, free from everything it represented, and finally free from Ken. When I saw the furniture he chose, I was shocked. He wanted to keep the nine gold-framed mirrors hanging in the house. It was evident to me how vain and self-absorbed he was. He believed he was the center of his own universe—a true narcissist.

Moving day arrived, and the attorneys agreed that Ken shouldn't be present while I moved out. However, an hour after the movers started, Ken showed up and walked in. Firmly, I told him, "You are not allowed to be here," and immediately called my lawyer, who advised me to video Ken inside the house.

Shortly after, Ken's phone rang. It was his lawyer instructing him to leave the house as he was violating our agreement. Ken drove off in his car, but to my surprise, twenty minutes later, he and David returned and walked in through the front door. Ken asserted, "I want to make sure you're not taking anything more than you're supposed to." Once again, I contacted my lawyer, and he advised me to continue videotaping Ken's violation of the court agreement.

As I began recording, Ken became highly agitated and insisted he wouldn't be kicked out of his own home. I calmly explained that I just wanted to move out peacefully and that he had promised not to interfere. Enraged, Ken approached and forcefully slapped the phone out of my hand. It wasn't his intention to hurt me; he simply didn't want to be filmed. It knocked me backward, and the phone struck my arm. Recognizing the severity of the situation, my attorney sought retribution and insisted I call 911. Unfortunately, the officers arrived after Ken and David had already left. I had a small bruise on my arm from the phone, so I took a photo of it as evidence.

The 911 call sent the Burnett family into a frenzy. Ken brazenly denied the incident, and his family, trusting his words, chose to believe him. Aunt Evie, the manipulative matriarch, had a meltdown. With the Burnett family connections to every judge in town, pursuing legal action seemed futile. Besides, compared to the beatings I endured from Logan, a bruise on my arm felt insignificant. My attorney was furious when I dropped the case, suggesting we bring criminal charges against Ken, but I was afraid. I knew Ken's family would wield their influence, burying me deeper in debt. I had no means to pay my mounting attorney fees. All I wanted was for the divorce to be settled so I could escape this exhausting battle.

The first night in my new home was a solitary one. After a day of unpacking, all I wanted was a hot bath and a cozy bed. The fear lurking within me prevented me from turning off most of the lights, and I made sure to activate the alarm. Fear consumed me, gnawing at my insides.

"No amount of money is worth this," I thought. I longed for the nightmare to end, to break free from Ken's grasping control. According to our settlement agreement, Ken was responsible for paying off my car and paying our health insurance. However, he had already canceled Emma's and my insurance- auto and medical. Ken had no urgency to settle the divorce; he wanted my legal fees to skyrocket. He had an endless supply of money to throw at the divorce proceedings, while I struggled to keep up. He had a safety net, while I teetered on the edge of financial ruin.

The day of my court appearance arrived, and I met my attorneys at their office. We rode together in their SUV to the courthouse. I wasn't particularly fond of my lawyer, but I had no choice but to continue with him. He was an old friend of my mother's, but I couldn't shake the feeling that he was prolonging the process to maximize his own financial gain. He showed no urgency in settling the case, racking up exorbitant fees along the way.

During the proceedings, the judge began dividing our debts and assigning them to both Ken and me. My share amounted to a staggering $250,000 in credit card debt which I was unaware of and half of the $750,000 mortgage. He even signed my name to a line of credit for $112,000 and pushed for joint custody of Emma without any obligation for child support, falsely claiming that I earned more money than him since he was unemployed. His convenient manipulation infuriated me. Sitting in the courtroom, I was overwhelmed by the realization that I was drowning in a million dollars of debt with no means to repay it. How could he be so cruel? We had been to Raymond James for financial investment advice for several years, Ken even lied to them about the level of our debt.

Realizing I couldn't change the situation, I decided to seek a settlement. The following day, I clandestinely met with a bankruptcy lawyer, an understanding older man who sympathized with my predicament. He explained that since I earned less than $32,000 now, I could declare bankruptcy and discharge my legal bills and marital debts. I met the criteria, prompting me to initiate the process immediately. It had to be completed before the divorce was finalized and my income increased as I took on the role of a loan officer.

The size of my legal fees was astronomical, colossal even. I had racked up a small fortune in legal bills so far, an absurd amount considering my lawyer hadn't achieved anything substantial for me. I knew he was milking the situation for all it was worth. Meanwhile, Ken had enlisted a formidable criminal defense lawyer who outperformed mine. Aunt Evie's influence over the judges was pervasive, ensuring that this divorce would never end favorably for me.

To everyone's surprise, I fired my lawyer, likely leaving him in shock when he discovered I had declared bankruptcy. Representing myself I signed divorce papers relinquishing any financial support from Ken or the Burnett family. Ken had threatened to take her away if I refused to forgo child support. Believing that he would prolong the legal battle indefinitely, I made the difficult decision to waive both alimony and child support, granting him joint custody. Forrest made me sign an NDA concerning anything that concerned the Burnett's and I was happy to do this in order to get Emma.

Although it felt like I was signing away my entire life, a newfound sense of freedom washed over me. At last, I was free from confinement. Free at last!

CHAPTER 21

Six months after my divorce was finalized, I found myself feeling isolated. So, I decided to seek the help of Belinda and Jo Ann in setting up dating profiles. Online matchmaking seemed weird and I wasn't sure if it was the right approach.

Jo Ann took charge of writing my profile, and as I read it, I couldn't help but laugh. It seemed so strange, and I wondered if it truly represented me. Belinda assured me that everyone was doing it and even shared stories of two women she knew who had found their second husbands through these platforms. As we scrolled through the profiles, Belinda suddenly exclaimed, "Look! Robyn Paxten is on here!" We all chuckled, and Belinda added, "The best part of starting over is never looking back."

The following day, I eagerly checked if anyone had viewed my profile. I received a couple of responses that caught my interest, so I arranged a lunch date with one of them. I thought lunch would be a safe option since I could use work as an excuse to leave early if needed. On the other hand, if I liked the person, I could plan drinks or dinner for another time. However, I quickly discovered that these men seemed to have ulterior motives.

During one lunch date, in the middle of our conversation, my date casually mentioned, "Kate, I do very well when I am on my medication." Intrigued, I asked about the condition he was taking medication for, to which he responded, "Bipolar Disorder." That revelation made me uncomfortable, so I blocked his calls after that.

Despite encountering some odd individuals, I refused to give up and spent many months engaged in phone conversations and exchanged emails, and just became bored with the details.

I shared with the girls that none of the men I met looked like their pictures and no one really interested me. I dubbed one guy "Liar, Liar Pants on Fire" because he turned out to be extremely short with a prominent gap in his front teeth, none of which was evident in his photos. When I told him I needed to use the restroom, I excused myself, walked straight to my car, and went home.

Maggie suggested that I give a Christian dating website a try, so I decided to give it a shot. However, I soon discovered that many of the guys on there weren't as "Christian" as they claimed to be. Casual sex seemed to be rampant among them, which was disappointing. It seemed like the dating scene had become all about short-term flings rather than finding a long-term commitment. I wanted a relationship, not just a casual encounter. It was disheartening. It made me remember my relationship with Jax was something real. We shared a close loving relationship with a profound connection, it was a bond that went beyond friendship marked by deep affection, trust, and understanding. Being in love with Jax in this way meant admiration and a desire for his happiness. God, I pray that he is happy.

I shared with Maggie that I felt the dating pool was shallow. At that point, I decided to go back to meeting dates at Starbucks to save myself time and effort. Some dates initially seemed promising, but then I would discover they had issues, no job, or they smelled strongly of incense. I did meet a few guys who appeared normal and continued to see them, hoping to get to know them better, but it felt like an uphill battle. Nothing really clicked. It was just a matter of time before I was apathetic.

Maggie told me that it seemed like no one could hold my attention. She was right. She reassured me, saying, "Kate, you are an elegant, beautiful woman who is well-polished. Don't give up." I agreed with her, stating that the next phase of my life had to be better than the first. Then Maggie told me Jax had been divorced for about a year. I was shocked and covered it by explaining Jax probably got divorced because he traveled all the time and was never around and I had not spoken to him in years. But I was careful to keep the longing to talk to him locked away, I would not speak about Jax. It was my turn to find happiness. Deep down, though, I felt the weight of desolation. I wondered what Jax was like now and what could have been. This was a thought that always bothered me. Love had only brought me pain thus far. So I hid my true feelings behind sarcasm and a playful sense of humor, always projecting a positive image to others, as if I hadn't lost my spark.

The one thing that kept me grounded was exercise. The gym became my sanctuary, where I could get away. It helped me maintain a more positive mindset and believe that my best days were still ahead of me.

One evening, when the girls and I gathered for dinner, they eagerly prodded me to share more of my dating adventures. Unfortunately, my friends seemed to be living vicariously through me and craved the stories. Speaking on behalf of everyone, Jo Ann urged me, saying, "Come on, Kate. Fill us in on the latest gems of male humanity that you've met."

I hammed it up and began telling them about a strikingly handsome man I had met for lunch. We hit it off, and he called me again for another outing. He seemed well put together and worked as a custom builder in town. One night, he took me to a party at a hotel where there was a DJ and everyone was dancing. Despite the loud music, I was actually having a good time, especially since he was a great dancer. After dancing for a while, we sat down to have a drink when another couple approached and asked if they could join us. Bob invited them to join us.

It was at that moment the other man asked how long we had been in the "lifestyle," to which I responded, "What do you mean?" He exchanged glances with his wife and then turned back to me, saying, "You don't know where you are, do you?" I was taken aback and admitted that I had no idea. He proceeded to explain that this was a swinger's party. I was utterly shocked! I turned to Bob, who said to the man, "She's vanilla." Bob then explained to me that "vanilla" meant I had not participated in the swinger lifestyle before.

As the girls shared their toast, Maggie, wide-eyed, asked me, "What did you do?" I explained that I was reassured by the couple at the swinger's party that there was no pressure, and I continued to have a few more drinks and dance. However, I never went out with Bob again. Casual sex and partner swapping were not my thing, and I was simply looking to meet someone new without getting involved in such a scene. Deciding to take a break from dating because it felt like a crazy and ever-changing dating world out there. I felt like my friends, being married for so long, couldn't fully grasp what it was like to be alone. Spending time alone just made me more picky. I refused to settle. The dating landscape had indeed changed since we were all in the dating game in college. While I had been open to new experiences, being a swinger had never crossed my mind. Being out from under Ken's narcissistic control was enough for now.

The girls raised their glasses and we had a toast, enjoying the opportunity to vent about the peculiarities of my past dating experiences. Belinda expressed her gratitude that she wasn't in my shoes, as she would have been completely freaked out.

I told the girls that after everything I had been through, I had reached a point where nothing fazed me anymore. I felt a sense of resilience and a willingness to embrace whatever life had in store for me.

Suddenly, Jo Ann interjected, "Alright. Who is going to tell her?" The others hesitated, and Belinda said, "Jo Ann, we said not tonight."

Confused, I asked them what they were talking about. Jo Ann then revealed, "Jax is going to have a photo exhibit in Asheville. He won an award for his photography!" I responded, "Was it for his photos documenting war-torn Syria?"

Realizing that I was already aware of the award, Maggie asked, "So you already knew?" I clarified, "I had heard about the award, but I wasn't aware of his exhibit."

Belinda added, "I don't think you ever forget your first love."

Feeling overwhelmed by talking about Jax, I quickly excused myself, explaining that I needed to go because Emma was home, and I wanted to stop by the grocery store. The truth was, I needed some time alone to process my emotions. No one really knew that I had been trying to keep up with Jax. Once I left, Jo Ann informed the other girls that Jax was probably not a topic of discussion, and that I just wasn't willing to talk about him.

When I arrived home, I prepared our favorite dinner, "chicken with goop," which consisted of chicken, Swiss cheese, and cream of chicken soup. It was our comfort food, ritz crackers on top. We then snuggled up together on the couch to watch the movie. Spending quality time with Emma helped me relax and let my guard down. She was gradually getting used to the visitation schedule and enjoyed spending time at both her dad's house and mine. David was nice to her, although he referred to me as "the starter wife," a term I despised.

As we watched the movie, thoughts of Ken crossed my mind. I had noticed him sitting alone during one of Emma's soccer games recently. It suddenly dawned on me that he must miss us. He must miss the couples we were friends with and the sense of family I had nurtured during every holiday, weekend, and dinner. I realized that Ken had lost more than I did. He had lost me.

In that moment, feeling a sense of satisfaction, knowing I had done everything for him. I was the ice-breaker, the buffer in social situations and made it comfortable for people to be around him. He lost all of his couple relationships, realizing that Ken might have felt incredibly lonely and missed the life we once had. His narcissistic ways made it even harder for him. We had been friends for many years, and he was someone I could shop with. We had shared good times and fun moments with our couple friends. Replacing long-term friendships is difficult, and Ken might never find that same connection again. On the other hand, I still had my girlfriends, Jill, and my mom.

Missing the time before I knew Ken was gay, and before I realized that he was indifferent to women. I missed the fantasy man I thought I was marrying. However, I hadn't lost anything significant except a man who never loved me. In a way, that was a blessing because it meant there was still hope for me. I didn't want revenge; I just wanted to embrace my life and find happiness. I did once care for Ken, as he was the father of my child, and that bond could never be broken. Yet, I longed to be loved and desired, to fill the empty void that gnawed at me. I genuinely enjoyed being married and wanted to be someone's wife. Living alone was something I disliked but it was better than being narcissistic supply.

To remind myself of the importance of happiness, I placed a quote by Robert Louis Stevenson on my bathroom mirror using tape so I could see it every day: "There is no duty we so much underrate as the duty of being happy."

Before I knew it, the weekend of Bele Chere had arrived. Bele Chere was a three-day music festival that attracted around 300,000 people each year. It offered a unique opportunity to experience the region's finest art, cuisine, and music.

Jill and Travis suggested that we all go to the street festival together so we could enjoy the vibrant atmosphere, listen to live music, and let loose. I wanted to dance to music and savor a glass of wine, while Travis looked forward to hearing his favorite country song playing, and Jill wanted to join in as a backup singer for any song she knew. Going out with Jill was always a lot of fun.

Asheville's Bele Chere, known as the largest outdoor festival in the Southeast, brought forth a vibrant atmosphere that rivaled the festivities of Mardi Gras in New Orleans. The collective spirit of the attendees was buoyant, as music reverberated through the streets and joyous crowds danced and mingled, blurring the boundaries between bars and the bustling thoroughfares.

During that particular year, Bele Chere unfolded as a lively and jam-packed affair. The attendees donned whimsical attire, filling the festival grounds with a colorful tapestry of costumes. Street musicians graced the air with their melodic tunes, while talented balloon artists fashioned impressive hats and playful animal creations. Laughter and merriment echoed in every corner.

Amidst the revelry, we came across a table arranged for whiskey pong, and the bar served a concoction intriguingly named the "Dirty Shirley," a libation we opted to avoid. Jill, my adventurous companion, ordered a drink for both of us and a beer for Travis. It was then that her eyes fixed upon a sizable group of men, prompting her to nudge me with a mischievous smile and say, "Now Kate, there is a table full of men that you need to be looking at."

Responding to Travis' gesture, our neighboring acquaintances joined our merry company, and he generously instructed the bartender to add their drinks to his tab. Our wine glasses never had a chance to empty, as the bartender diligently refilled them, leaving Jill and me blissfully unaware of just how much wine we were consuming.

As the evening wore on, Jill's joyful mood soared, leading her to dispense marital advice to a nearby couple who were celebrating their anniversary. In her exuberance, she even showered Travis with affectionate kisses. The festival proved to be a haven for music lovers, with live performances and impromptu jam sessions abounding in every nook and cranny. Meanwhile, I delighted in engaging in lively conversations with our amiable neighbors.

Jill, with her unabating determination, was not one to let an opportunity pass. Urging me forward, she goaded me to approach the group of men at the table. Summoning my courage, I marched over and boldly declared, "I am single, and my sister dared me to come over here." To my surprise, one of the men kindly informed me, "Well… This is probably not the best table for you. Every year, we meet here… and we're all gay." Realizing the situation, I swiftly retrieved Jill, linking her arm with mine, and led her to the table. Introductions were made, and the gentleman repeated his revelation to Jill. Laughter ensued, sealing our shared understanding that such serendipitous encounters were unique to Bele Chere.

We ventured outside for a leisurely stroll, relishing the ambiance and taking in the sounds of an indie band performing nearby. Eventually, we returned to the welcoming embrace of the bar's lively interior. Travis, spotting a golfing buddy, engaged in animated conversations and shared anecdotes, while the bar patrons enjoyed in the festive night. Travis had no idea that "a condor" was a hole in one on a five par. Amidst the animated chatter and the pulsating energy of the vibrant nightlife, the air was thick with celebration.

At one point, a fellow bar-goer espoused his belief in extraterrestrial life, finding the topic immensely intriguing. Quick-witted as ever, Jill rolled her eyes. Clearly, Jill had consumed enough to embrace a playful sense of mischief. As the night wore on the bar continued to brim with people happily partaking in the revelries. There was an unparalleled allure to this festival, a palpable sense of collective celebration hanging in the air.

My gaze drifted to Jill, only to find her engrossed in a phone call. I pointed out that Travis was just across the room, but she nonchalantly claimed to be dialing the Hotel Indigo in search of Jax. Concerned, I warned her, "No, you're not! In a slurred state, Jill defiantly proclaimed, "I left him a message." It was evident that the drinks had taken their toll.

The catchy beats filled the air, and I managed to coax Jill onto the dance floor. Jill, an endearing yet inept dancer, had me doubled over in laughter. The more she tried, the more amusing her dance moves became. In that moment, amidst the laughter, I reveled in the sheer delight of being in the presence of my beloved older sister.

Leaving the dance floor, Jill gestured for me to join her at the bar, where we struck up a conversation with a neighboring couple, Dan and his wife. Dan, an affable and humorous individual, regaled us with jokes and anecdotes. It was in the midst of this jovial exchange that Jill caught sight of Jax entering the bar. His thick, wavy hair framed his face in a way that seemed effortlessly styled and irresistibly tousled. Every gesture he made carried an air of grace and strength as if he were always in control, yet humble enough to put others at ease. His broad shoulders and sculpted physique spoke to discipline yet, beneath the surface there was a gentleness that softened his rugged exterior. With sudden fervor, Jill pushed her way through the crowd, determined to confront Jax. Travis, witnessing the commotion, hurried over to intervene, questioning Jill's actions. In a belligerent tone, she exclaimed to the gathered crowd, "This is Jax."

Puzzled, Travis inquired, "So why are you trying to hit him?" Jill's response pierced the air, resonating above the clamor of the crowd, "Because Kate still loves him, she always has." Amidst the chaos, Travis lovingly embraced Jill, guiding her towards the dance floor, his words expressing both affection and amusement: "It is such a privilege to watch your mind at work."

Lost in the whirlwind of emotions and events, I heard my name being called. Turning, I beheld Jax slowly making his way towards me, a familiar grin adorning his face, igniting a long- dormant spark within me. He did look handsome with sexy wind- tossed hair. Reminded of the chemistry we had as he looked at me with his blue eyes, electricity surged through the air. Time seemed to stand still as we exchanged knowing smiles. Every time he smiled at me like that, it knocked me off my feet all over again. My heart raced, and the familiar butterflies fluttered in my stomach. Jax made his way toward me, his steps filled with a mix of hesitation and excitement. Our embrace was all-consuming, reaffirming the connection we had shared. The years melted away as we felt the chemistry that once was there, leaving no room for doubt.

I whispered, "Jax, why did you come here."

"To find you," said Jax

"Please, come see the exhibition tomorrow," Jax replied

And a laugh came from me filled with nervousness, heartache, and joy.

"You have a great laugh," he said.

In that crowded bar, on the bustling dance floor where our paths had intertwined once again, we agreed to meet the next day.

Walking around the art exhibit that was blooming with vibrant colors, I'm impressed by seeing beautiful photos blown up and displayed everywhere. Among the throngs of art enthusiasts, I was looking for his familiar face. Then, in the center of the whole exhibit, I see it…the photo of me that Jax took in the field of yellow flowers. Moving to it mesmerized I see it's called: NUGGET. I put my hand over my mouth and gasp.

"It's always been my favorite," Jax said standing close. So I wheel around and Jax is standing in front of me. The air crackled with an unspoken recognition. His words hung delicately in the space between us, as if hesitant to break the connection of the moment. A grin graced his eyes, and he stood tall commanding attention with his presence. His chiseled jawline accentuated his confident smile, drawing me to him.

"Hi, Nugget." He said.

"Hi," I said. It felt good to see his broad chest and muscular frame but it was his charisma that made him truly handsome.

Jax asked, "Would you like to ride out to see that field again for old times' sake?

"Why," I said while my pulse was racing.

"You know why," Jax smiled, "My feelings for you never stopped."

Jax held up three fingers. I. Love. You.

I did know why. This time I let the tears come. But tears of joy. I held up three fingers. Our eyes met, and a rush of emotions flooded my heart. In that moment we realized how much we missed each other and the sparks that had been reignited. Laughter, shared memories, and a sense of familiarity enveloped us like a warm embrace. We knew deep down that we were meant to be together. The experiences we gained apart had shaped us into stronger individuals, ready to embark on a new chapter as a reunited couple. Jax said the love he felt was even more profound now, having overcome the challenges of distance and growth.

After years of being apart, navigating their separate paths, fate intervened to bring Jax and me back together. We decided to cherish every moment and rediscover the depths of our affection. With each passing season, our love blossomed, surpassing the memories of our high school romance and we embraced the present, appreciating the maturity and depth that our time apart had cultivated within us.

Jax faced a pivotal choice concerning his promising career, he knew he could not bear another separation.

We grew stronger as a couple and God mended the broken pieces in each of us. The closeness we found with each other is only something most people dream about. Marrying your best friend is the start to a beautiful life. Jax is my other half and I was lost without him. You hope that love is your destiny and Jax was my journey toward a loyal relationship.

Emma attended college in North Carolina and had a fun normal experience. She grew into her own life. Emma decided to search for her birth parents and found her birth mother first. She was quickly told that she wanted nothing to do with Emma because she was married with 3 children and never told her husband about Emma being born. So for a while Emma carried this rejection around from her birth mother. I believe the lies her birth mother told finally caught up to her but deep down I'm grateful she chose adoption over abortion because that gave me a daughter. Emma eventually found the other side of her birth family and those relationships grew and flourished. It was very healing for Emma to explore and embrace these relationships. The love and acceptance she found was beyond what she could have imagined.

I had friends who were shocked that I was so comfortable with Emma searching and finding her birth family. My answer to them was, "You can't have too many people love you and I am Emma's mom and nothing will ever change that."

Emma and I spent time separately in therapy healing from the trauma we faced and used therapy to navigate the narcissistic abuse we experienced from Ken. Unless you have experienced emotional abuse it's hard to explain the anger that comes from realizing you allowed yourself to be manipulated, used and targeted by someone who is incapable of love. Therapy helped me understand the insidious scars that narcissistic abuse leaves behind. God threw me a life raft but expected me to row. God expected me to participate in my own rescue. Jax and I traveled the world for four years while he took photos. He also took photos for the government as well but he could not tell me much about that. That's another story. Probably the reason he stayed out of contact for so long. We made a decision to pursue our dreams together, supporting each other every step of the way. We then got married in Israel at the church in Cana where Jesus turned water into wine. Jax always wanted to retire on a lake so we moved to a lake in the mountains of North Carolina. The view is so pretty with the sun sparkling on the water looking across at the trees on the mountains. As a couple, we overcame every obstacle and built trust with each other. Our relationship centers around laughter. Jax is the only man who I ever let in, or who I believed worthy to let my own walls down. He's the only man I would ever fight for. Jax and I became an inspiration-a testament to the enduring power of love and the significance to second chances. Our story became one of commitment, resilience and unwavering belief in the power of love. We proved that even though life's circumstances may pull people apart, destiny has a way of bringing people back together, stronger than ever before. Cherish the past, embrace the present, and hold on to the person who makes your heart feel complete.

www.ingramcontent.com/pod-product-compliance
Lightning Source LLC
Chambersburg PA
CBHW030133010826
48973CB00002B/545